REBIRTH

HAVOK
SEASON ONE

REBIRTH

HAVOK: SEASON ONE

A Flash Fiction Anthology

EDITOR-IN-CHIEF
ANDREW WINCH

For information, contact Havok Publishing:
https://gohavok.com
publishing@gohavok.com

ISBN: 978-1-0750-3102-1
First paperback edition July 2019

Printed in the United States of America

CONTENTS

Introduction 1

When Magic Died / Michael Dolan 3

Life Cycle 63 / Just B. Jordan 7

Sins Of Fire And Metal / Emileigh Latham 11

Fourth Time's the Charm / J. L. Ender 15

The Feathered Corpse / Bill Bibo, Jr. 20

Three Wishes / James Scott Bell 24

The Doomsday Stones / Jebraun Clifford 28

Bitten / Jessi L. Roberts 32

The Choice / Kaitlyn Emery 35

The Misfits / Samwise Graber 39

Gilded Finality / Brianna Tibbetts 43

Every Drop of Soul / Lila Kims 45

Run / Cathy Hinkle 49

Seeing is Believing / Clarissa Ruth 53

One Last Time / Robert Liparulo 57

Unnatural 20 / Andrew Swearingen 61

Dune Buggy Dash / Katie Robles 65

Ordained / Tracey Dyck 69

If These Walls Could Talk / J. L. Knight 73

Corruption's Kiss / Margaret Graber 75

Proteus / Kerry Nietz 79

To Find a Thief / E. A. West 84

Humdinger's Army / A. C. Williams 88

A Terrible Debtor / Savannah Grace 92

Misfire / Abigayle Claire 95

Ghost of The Golf Course / Kristiana Y. Sfirlea 99

The Tomb of the Ophidian Scepter / Michael Dolan 102

My Brother the Office Chair / Rosemary E. Johnson 106

One Shot / Zachary Holbrook 110

The Devil Went Down to Costco / Stephanie Scissom 114

Life Lessons from Grandpa / DiAnn Mills **117**

Baubles and Beads / Lisa Godfrees 122

At Your Service / Christine Smith 126

Window / Carie Juettner 131

Salvage and Reclamation / Abigail Falanga 134

It's Going To Be Okay / Teddi Deppner 139

An Undeserved Chance / Justin Mynheir 143

The Cleaner / R. C. Capasso 147

Born to Ruin / David Farland **150**

Dino Day / Lauren Hildebrand 154

Words / Katherine Vinson 158

Rendering / L. G. McCary 161

Finnegan Transmitting / Eva Schultz 166

A New Ridill / Andrew Winch 170

The Pet Rock Named Dave / Justin Mynheir 174

The Candy Conspiracy / E. A. West 178

Recluse / Lauren H. Salisbury 182

A Symphony of Words / Kerry Nietz 186

About Our Authors 192

OUR EDITORS

MYSTERY MONDAY:
Lisa Godfrees
Karen deBlieck

TECHNO TUESDAY:
Steve Rzasa
Rachel Harris

WACKY WEDNESDAY:
Lauren Hildebrand
Gen Gavel

THRILLER THURSDAY:
Cathy Hinkle
Savannah Grace

FANTASY FRIDAY:
Andra Marquardt

COPY EDITORS:
Elizabeth Liberty Lewis
Lauren Salisbury

EDITOR-IN-CHIEF:
Andrew Winch

For the Havok Horde,
and with everlasting admiration
for the Havok Hive.

Special thanks to our Season One
*Patreon Firebrand: **Kaitlyn Emery**.*
It's true believers like you who
set the stories free to fly.

INTRODUCTION

Havok. Maybe this is the first time you've seen the name. Maybe you've read a few of our free stories on **GoHavok.com.** Or maybe you belong to our Horde—voting, commenting, sharing, and following our journey. However this little anthology comes to you, you should know that it's significant.

Rebirth isn't just a theme. It's a legacy.

An embodiment of enduring spirit. You see, at the end of 2018, *Havok Magazine* died. And it almost stayed dead.

But a passion for flash fiction and for our community of authors inspired a few of us to forge ahead. And fueled by this inspiration, Havok Publishing rose from the ashes. With a long list of overly ambitious goals and tight deadlines to drive us, we grew our staff to more than two-dozen highly dedicated volunteers and launched something brand new in January 2019.

After six months, this anthology is the carefully curated culmination of hundreds of submitted stories and a few that we specifically hunted down. After all, every party is more exciting with some superstars in the mix.

Whether you're here because your brother's story made the cut or because you want to check out an exclusive flash fiction by one of your favorite authors, we think you'll enjoy the ride, cover to cover.

Why? Because we've combined six months of themes (rebirth,

recycle, relocate, reform, recover, and redo) with five of the most popular fiction genres (mystery, sci-fi, comedy, thriller, and fantasy) to bring you original, entertaining, thought provoking stories that will leave an impact long after you're done reading them.

And who knows? Maybe you, too, will be reborn somewhere along the way.

Andrew Winch / Lisa Godfrees / Teddi Deppner
aka Cerberus

WHEN MAGIC DIED

By Michael Dolan

Throughout the entirety of Dave's quest, he'd seen the signs and heard the whispers that magic was dying. And just when he reached the island at the edge of the world, it had the nerve to do just that.

Four dragons watched him upend his backpack beside the small tree on the cliff top. He rifled through spilled food, potions, enchanted weapons, and cursed artifacts collected on his quest to find and place seven mana gems on the tree's outstretched boughs.

As he placed the last gem, a thunderous crack split the air. They flared bright for a second before quickly corroding and winking out.

"Missed it by that much," intoned the viridian dragon.

Dave looked up at the four beasts gathered around. "What does that mean?"

"Magic has died, brave champion," answered the crimson dragon. "Though noble, your quest has failed."

"Fat lot of help you were," muttered Dave.

The cerulean dragon turned toward him. "What was that?"

"Um, just 'That's not a healthy picture.'"

"Indeed not," said the golden dragon. "Magic is already

3

receding across the realm. But even in its death, the promise of new life remains."

"Come again?" said Dave.

"Though you failed to reunite the mana tree with its lost fruit before it perished, you still have a part to play in shaping the future of magic. When the tree and the magic within pass away, you will help craft its very foundation in the coming age." The golden dragon breathed a jet of fire at the small tree. The blaze caught, enveloped the tree in a pillar of flame, and reduced it to ash.

The three other dragons looked at one another. "Was that... necessary?" asked the viridian dragon.

"Did you want to wait around for who knows how long for it to wither by itself?" The golden dragon released a snort of smoke. "I have better things to do than literally watch a plant slowly die, no matter how magical."

"My vote's with him," interjected Dave.

The cerulean dragon rolled its eyes and reached into the ashes. It lifted out a heavy tome and passed it to Dave. "As magic is reborn, let its laws be rewritten."

The champion accepted the volume. The cover was undecorated, so he turned it over to see if there was anything on the back. Finding nothing, he rotated it to look at the spine. Empty again. He inspected the edges of the pages before slowly leafing through, though they seemed just as blank. He closed the book and studied the cover again. A dragon coughed politely.

Dave looked up. Four intense, draconic faces stared back. He blanched with embarrassment. "What's this for again?"

The crimson dragon shifted its wings. "As champion of the last age, it is your right and responsibility to dictate the laws of magic upon its rebirth."

Dave squinted and glanced from dragon to dragon.

"A magic system," the dragon clarified. "You're supposed to come up with a magic system."

"Ohhh." Dave nodded slowly. He glanced down at the book. "You know, rules aren't really my strength. How about we just let magic do its own thing this time, figure it'll sort itself out eventually?"

The dragons laughed a deep, collective rumble that lingered in the air. The golden one spoke. "That may have worked in the past, when magic wasn't as deeply studied as it is today. But we live in a more civilized age. People expect it to follow rules, to have defined sources, effects, and costs. Magic must be balanced and predictable. If not, it just becomes too overpowered."

"Makes sense," said Dave. "After all, we can't have magic getting too—what's the word?—magical, right?"

The cerulean dragon narrowed its eyes and raised a scaly eyebrow. "We're going to forget you said that. Look, it's not that hard. You can make this system as simple as you want. Just base it off symbols, or the elements, or physics or something."

"Or flavors," said the viridian dragon.

"Would you stop suggesting that every time we do this?" said the cerulean dragon. "It's a horrible idea for a magic system."

"You're just jealous of my refined palate."

"Or you could choose song," said the golden dragon, obviously trying to cut short an argument it'd heard far too many times.

Dave laughed. "Enchanted karaoke? Not on my watch."

"How about incantations?"

Dave shook his head. "Not unless it's igpay atinlay."

"Smells?"

"I'd say your flavors idea was better."

"Well you have to pick something," said the golden dragon. "And you must choose soon."

"Why? Magic is dead. It's not exactly going anywhere."

"True, but its ability to regenerate is waning. If you don't write something down soon, the only things magic will be good for is tying your shoes and making enemies itch in places they can't quite reach."

"Okay, okay. I'll come up with something." Dave opened the book. "How am I supposed to write in this anyway?"

"The laws of magic must be inscribed with the champion's blood," recited the crimson dragon.

Said blood drained from Dave's face.

"Haha, just kidding. Use the ash from the burnt tree."

"Seriously?"

"Yes."

Dave walked to the pile of ash, sat down, and opened the tome. "This is so unsanitary." He dipped his finger into the residue and began writing.

Time passed. Leaving Dave to write in peace, the dragons entertained themselves with games of tic tac toe and dots and boxes. When at last the champion closed the book, the golden dragon looked up. "Have you finished?"

"Noo." Dave rolled his eyes. "I just like the sound of books closing." He disappeared into thin air.

The confused dragons looked at one another, then walked over to where Dave had been sitting. The tome's cover lay open, revealing its handwritten title page: *The Magical Laws of Snark and Sarcasm.*

The dragons looked at one another with wide eyes. "Huh," the viridian one said as they sat back on their haunches. "This'll be interesting."

LIFE CYCLE 63

EDITOR'S CHOICE * By *Just B. Jordan*

Dirt encroached on the window, etched into the pane by the force of three hundred fifteen days and twenty thousand wings.

The delascopics tracked Mateo's target, slowing time within its eyepiece. It was day sixty-three of the planet's life cycle. Tomorrow would be day one again. Today was their fourth run.

The empty clanking of boots on metal invaded *Temerity's* disfigured bay. Mateo glanced away from the delascopics, silently greeting the rest of his team. Stefek still looked pale and fevered. He distributed specimen jars to the other two. Kiana carried a jagged pole as a cane. Her cybernetic eyes hadn't survived the shrapnel from their crash. Then there was Farid, who had been their runner. The edges of his splint ticked against the floor like the hands of a cruel clock.

"Rate?" Stefek said.

"Two hundred wingbeats per minute."

None of them wore enviro suits. *Temerity's* fall had created a breach in its hull, sucking the suits and most of their tools out before they could seal it.

Mateo pulled stale, filtered air through his nose. Slow. Steady.

"You'll have three minutes to gather, at best," Farid said. "You're not as fast as I was. Do you remember my map?"

Mateo wouldn't have time to look at a copy while he ran. "Mental perfect."

Farid handed him a sack. "Find parts and tools—our provisions can stretch for one more cycle."

"Rate?" Stefek said.

"One hundred fifty."

A mound of earth pressed against the outer rim of the window. *Temerity* had not crashed softly. A stretch of blackened earth extended from her hull, then clusters of rock and a few stubborn tree spines more charcoal than wood. Beyond that, his goal, kissed by the satin blue of sky and everything made of stars.

"Rate?" Stefek whispered.

Mateo kept his gaze trained through the delascopics. Ten thousand black and orange butterflies cut the sky to patches. Their rate per minute lowered, as did the height of their swarm. The churning changed. Softened.

The first one dropped.

Mateo held the delascopics out to Stefek. "Ninety."

More of the creatures fell. Their wings dusted up grains of old ash, obscuring their colors. Mateo moved to the hanger door.

"Kiana, take soil again," Stefek said. "Farid, samples of plant life."

Mateo crouched, leaning forward to brush a knuckle of his glove against *Temerity's* side. "I'll make it back." Stale, filtered breaths. Deep. Steady. "Rate?"

"All down. Winds are dead. Environment safe in thirty, twenty nine—"

Mateo closed his eyes. One run. One step closer to healing *Temerity*.

"Zero."

The hanger door opened with a squeal of torqued metal. Dirt slid toward Mateo's shoes. He ran.

Death didn't chase him. It surrounded him. It was just dormant for the next twenty minutes.

Wings crushed under his feet, their life completed. Mateo

only had until the next one began. He tried to calm his heartrate. One mile.

It took eight minutes.

Mateo leaped down a hill, landing amid pieces of *Temerity's* exterior. Some preserved food littered the area. Perishables had rotted months ago. He hurried through twisted lengths of metal, grabbing the provisions in easy reach. He didn't see a single enviro suit amid the wreckage.

A hint of red. The tech box. Its latch was popped. Mateo's hands fumbled, searching through the scattered tools, throwing some in his sack. Most of them weren't critical to *Temerity's* repairs. Then he found a net drive and a coil of unused ebon wire. These, they needed. He slid his arm through the loop of wire so it wouldn't crush, and turned toward home. Time was closing.

Ten minutes left.

He stepped on a ridged lump. The EL generator. It looked whole.

That could get *Temerity* working again.

He heaved it out of the earth. It wasn't large, but it was weighted. His fingers found a handle, and he ran.

Nine minutes to get home.

The sound of paper slowly tearing.

Desperation clawed from Mateo's throat, pushing him faster. *Temerity* wasn't in sight. He was surrounded by plant life dotted with cocoons.

Hundreds of them.

All slowly cracking open.

The barest breeze put a sway in the green of the world. The wind returned, bringing the beginning of this planet's next life cycle—and the toxins—with it.

Mateo careened out of the forest, into a field of charcoal spines. *Temerity.*

One minute.

His team stood in the open hanger door, specimens collected and sealed. Stefek and Farid shouted at the sight of the EL generator. They'd all assumed it would be in pieces.

Thirty seconds. The warning pulsed shrill from within *Temerity*. Stefek had programed its doors to remain open for twenty minutes. No overrides. They would close automatically.

Mateo let go of the generator. A dozen dead butterflies shifted at its impact. Sweat and tears blurred his vision.

His legs seized. He stumbled toward *Temerity*. Toward home, broken as it was.

Twenty seconds.

Mateo pulled the wire off his arm, dropping it in the sack. He sealed its mouth and threw it.

Five seconds.

The bag cleared the doors, landing at Kiana's feet.

A screech of metal. A screech of soul.

Mateo stood in a field of ash, looking at dirt etched into a window pane by the force of three hundred fifteen days and twenty thousand wings. There were three faces. All screaming, the thump of their fists reverberating from within *Temerity's* hull.

One hand spread across the glass, as if to feel what she could not see. Mateo stepped forward. His legs burned. His eyes burned.

The air burned.

The distant trees blinked in color—ten thousand newborn butterflies drying their wings on a toxic breeze. Ten yards away, the EL generator.

Mateo pointed at it. His hand shook. "Sixty-three more days." He felt his lungs corroding. "Then you will have enough power to put our home back in the stars."

A butterfly landed on his shoulder.

SINS OF FIRE AND METAL

By Emileigh Latham

An electric pulse jerks my muscles awake. I gasp, filling my lungs with air. My heart pounds against my chest as it rushes me back to life.

A robotic voice announces. "Engine's Power Level: Low. Light Speed: Unavailable."

"Quickly, human fenix! Fire up the ssship," demands a huffing, hissing voice.

Does he think this is easy? Dying and then coming back to life, again and again?

An explosion tears through the hull, and the ship convulses from the blast. My body lifts then falls, slamming against my cot. Slumping to the floor, I wheeze as my lungs burn from the exertion.

Flinching at the shrieking alarms, I shift to my side and strain to lift myself off the frigid steel floor. The smell of smoke filters into the cabin.

"We've been hit! Hurry up, boy! Ussse your flame to ignite the engine." The snake-like voice comes from Occa, my prison guard.

A stronger pulse burns through me. I scream until my voice cracks.

A new voice yells, "Occa! Why hasn't the human charged up

the engine?"

The hot current sizzling through me ceases. I crumble back onto the freezing floor and press myself against it, trying to convince my trembling body to be as solid as the metal beneath me.

"Human fenix?" That's the captain, my master. My eyes begin to focus. Old battle scars run down his purple-skinned face. His teal-colored hair and goatee glow like the embers of the cig in his mouth.

My vision spins and my middle coils. Turning to my side, I heave the meager contents of my stomach.

"Occa, you reptilian slime." I hear a hiss escape Occa's lips as the captain kicks Occa through the energy shield that cages me. "The human is worth a fortune. Possibly more than ten of your lifetimes with how rare its flame is. If you've damaged it—"

I raise myself. My hand slips under me, and I sink back to the floor, shaking.

What's the point, anyways? This is what I deserve.

"We need to get out of here, human, if we are to escape Red Eye and his armada." The cig in his mouth warps his words.

Red Eye? He's here?

A different kind of chill slithers its way through me, and I feel my power smoldering in my chest again.

He found me.

I push myself up into a sitting position, panting from the effort.

I must help them escape.

I bow my head at the captain.

"How long will you be out after this?" he asks me.

Even though I am precious equipment, I am a slave. My station is lower than a crew member. No sense in accusing Occa of weakening me. "I'll be unconscious for a couple of days, master."

If I'm lucky, maybe forever.

The captain steps through the energy shield. "Understood. Ignite the engine, human. Occa, tell the pilot we're launching in 20 seconds."

One side of Occa's green, scaly face glows as he opens the communication link between the crew and repeats the captain's orders.

I pull myself up onto my feet using my cot, and wobble. Putting the wall at my back to keep me standing, I raise my hands and expel blue flame. The room around me begins to charge and absorb the fire. I hear the purr of the engine as it eats up my power. Taking a deep inhale of hot air, I reach inside and break the barrier within. Power surges through my body as a sapphire inferno engulfs me. My fingers turn to dust. I press on, relieving myself of all the raging energy. I taste my ashes as more of me turns. When my eyes evaporate into embers, it is then that my sin dances into view, haunting me. There was one person who never gave up on me, and when I ignited in front of him, I melted his flesh and blasted his arm off.

I feel the cold sleep of death consume me. I hope it is for the last time.

I choke as crisp, cold water washes over me. I gulp in air, and my heart jumps into action. I sit up this time and see the face I have dreaded seeing again.

"Red Eye."

His cybernetic eye glints. "Hello, brother."

I do nothing but stare at my cyborg brother, gazing at what I had done to him.

He sets the bucket down and clears his throat. "The whole crew is either dead or captured. Or do you care, Jaco, since you were just a slave?"

I remain still. Hearing my name after so long takes me back to the last time I heard it. He was lying in my arms, whispering my name over and over. His body mutilated because of me.

"Why did you run away?"

I stay silent, not caring for this conversation. My soul died a long time ago. Living no longer matters.

"Do you know why I have been searching for you?" His cyborg eye glows a deeper red.

"You found a way to kill me." I sigh. "Just do it. I have longed for death. Take your revenge."

He lowers himself and brings his face close to mine. A tear runs down his good eye. "I don't want to kill you, Jaco. I am here to pardon you. It was an accident."

I hold my breath.

"After I heard of your capture, I went to the emperor and convinced him to form an armada against fenix slave ships so that I could find you and end your oppression. I prayed that I would one day free you from your bondage."

"I never thought..." I release the breath I was holding. "I am so sorry." My face is wet again from tears I didn't realize I was shedding.

"I forgive you, little brother." He lifts me up onto my feet and embraces me. "Let's go home."

FOURTH TIME'S THE CHARM

By J. L. Ender

I hit the concrete so hard it shattered beneath me.

"Disappointing." Phantom Lad shook his head. He floated several feet above me, blue energy pulsing from his hands. "I expected more."

You and me both.

Onlookers, the ones who didn't flee in terror, aimed their phones at us. I stared up into powder-blue heavens framed by skyscrapers. Body broken, I coughed up a wad of blood and died.

⋯⋯⋯⋯⋯⋯⋯⋯⋯⋯⋯⋯⋯⋯

I hurtled toward Earth, plummeting from the York Banking building. Empire City spread beneath me—a loud, chaotic jumble of buildings, cars, and people. I caught myself on a stone parapet, scraping skin from my palms. Muscles quivering, I hauled my exhausted body onto a balcony.

Phantom Lad crashed into me. We smacked against the windows of the building. I threw a flaming punch at the villain, but he blocked it with a barrier of light, then delivered a vicious kick to my face. My teeth clacked as I smashed through glass, tumbling onto the carpeted floor of an office.

Stunned, body lacerated in dozens of places, I lay there, trying to gather my wits. Before I could rise, my adversary created a blade of blue energy and plunged it into my chest. A sense of peace overcame me, then... death.

I sprinted across the rooftop, wind whistling in my ears. My cape flapped behind me, tugged by strong gusts.

Phantom Lad laughed. "You're too late, Fire Wolf! The bomb's in Chicago. You picked the wrong city!"

I created a ball of fire in my right hand and hurled it at him. He raised an energy blade and sliced the ball in half, then spun and threw the blade at me. I shrouded myself in fire, melting the roof's blacktop while destroying the projectile.

With a sigh, he pulled out a pistol and shot me in the gut. I dropped to my knees in the mushy asphalt.

"That's..." I gasped, unable to finish the sentence as my gut spasmed with pain.

"Not fair?" Phantom Lad chuckled. "I'm the bad guy. It's what we do."

He floated in front of me and pointed his gun at my head. A bang, a red flash, then... death.

"No, no. This is all wrong. Why does this fool keep dying *sooner?*" The voice was familiar, but I couldn't place it.

"It's almost like we shouldn't meddle with time..." I could swear I'd heard *this* voice before, too.

"Hello?" I called into darkness.

"We were *told* not to mess with the time stream more than once, after all," the second voice continued. Fuzzy memories ran through my head. Memories of dying...

"Semantics! Bygones! Puddleducks!"

"None of that makes any sense."

"What's done is done. We're here. How do we fix this?"

"It might not *be* fixable."

"He's got the potential to be a great hero. Let's try once more. If he still dies, we give up."

"Hello?" I tried again.

The voices ignored me. "Once more," the second one said. "But that's it!"

I raced toward York Banking. "You're in place?" I asked Zap-Girl.

"We're disarming the bomb now. You were right. He *did* plant it in Chicago! At Willis Tower!"

"Okay. Time to deal with Phantom Lad. Talk soon."

"Don't go alone! Wait for backup!"

"I'll be fine. It's Phantom Lad. We've dealt with him a hundred times before."

"But a bomb? He's never gone this far before. Be careful, Wolfie. You're not invincible."

"You know me, babe. Careful is my middle name. Fire *Careful* Wolf."

Wishing I could fly straight up, I rode the elevator to the top floor.

Phantom Lad waited, standing perfectly balanced on the railing with a deadly drop mere centimeters away.

He laughed. "You're too late, Fire Wolf!"

He's going to shoot you.

Grin collapsing, he pulled out a gun. I stepped to the side and hurled a head-sized fireball at him as the bullet whizzed by. *How did I know about the gun?*

Phantom Lad dodged, but lost balance. His arms wind-milled,

and he dropped the gun as he fell backward. I bolted forward, grabbed his wrist with both hands, and braced my feet against the railing.

"You saved me?" he asked. "Why?"

"I'm a hero." I gritted my teeth, hauling him onto the balcony. "It's what we do."

"How did you know I wouldn't be able to fly?"

"We've studied your powers. We know you need a running start."

He seemed to contemplate this. "You could have let me die."

"Like I said..."

"I would have let *you* die," he went on, louder. "I was going to kill you."

Two men stepped from the elevator. Aside from a height difference, their bald heads and green robes made them nearly indistinguishable.

"I told you we just needed one more!" the shorter man said. "Fourth time's the charm!"

"You did not. You had no idea." The taller man rolled his eyes.

"Who are you?" I was certain I'd seen them before. Their voices were so familiar.

"We've traveled to this primitive time to make sure things proceed as they should," the shorter man said.

I straightened my spine. "I'm honored, but really—"

"Not you," the shorter man interrupted, pointing at Phantom Lad. "Him."

"He'll commit terrible crimes," the tall one continued, "and we traced his descent to this day. We thought if we could change the outcome—change his fate—we'd fix the future."

The taller man held his hand out to Phantom Lad. "And now, if you'll come with us, we have much more we would teach you."

Phantom Lad took the outstretched palm, and the three

vanished.

"Well… that was weird." I told the empty rooftop.

Leaning against the railing, I sighed, gazing down at the city below. *Saved you again, and not even a thank you.* But that was nothing new. Sometimes being a superhero was about the smaller rewards.

"Fire Wolf!" Zap-Girl cried. "You ok?"

"Yep," I said. "Just enjoying the view."

THE FEATHERED CORPSE

By Bill Bibo, Jr.

In a world where mythical creatures lived and worked alongside a human population, anything could happen, and it usually did. That's why they called me, Special Agent Ramses II, and my partner, Bernie Clayberg, with Mythical Crime Scene Investigations.

The alley was a narrow space filled with police bumping into one another like a bad game of pinball. I followed Bernie in. One of the benefits of having a golem as your partner was that even in the most crowded situations, people cleared a wide path. At least they had better. And when you had the brittle bones of a mummified Egyptian pharaoh, that was a necessity.

On one side, a group of detectives interviewed a mild-mannered human male. He was trying to answer their questions while blubbering into a handkerchief. On the other waited Chief Inspector Krupke and his junior officer Carl Yaztremski, both of the Rainbow City Police Department.

"Hey, Carl, what's a mummy's favorite music?" Krupke said as we approached.

"I don't know, Chief," Carl answered. "Wrap music?"

Krupke's eyes narrowed, probably a warning not to steal his punchlines. "No, idiot, it's Ragtime."

"Nice to see you too, Krupke," I said. "Where's the body?"

"That's why we called. We had a body..."

"What do you mean?"

"It's gone." Krupke led us to a taped off area. "We got a call. Someone heard a scream, then gunshots. When we got here, we found pretty boy over there gleefully dancing in the alley. Then we see the body. A young woman, hands and feet bound, seven gunshots. When he sees us, the guy starts to cry. Says he didn't kill her. No priors, not even a parking ticket."

"Why call MCSI?"

"My squad's taking photos, gathering info, when there's this big bright flash like the air around us is on fire. Only lasted a second and it's gone. Only thing, so's the body. All that's left is a pile of ashes and this." He hands me an evidence bag with a long black feather in it. "I can't deal with this. Dead human bodies don't go all blazing out in glory."

"If the body disintegrated in flames, why not this feather?" I turned to Krupke. "Mind if I take this?"

"Might as well. Without a body, I'm not sure I have a case."

We walked over to where the suspect was sitting. I left Bernie standing next to him while I looked for anything that might help make sense of what happened.

The man was nervous. He tried to engage Bernie in conversation, but Bernie just stood there, perfectly doing his thing—standing mute and motionless. When we were again alone in the car Bernie spoke, "He kept muttering over and over that he didn't kill anyone, that it was her job. Mentioned something about meeting her at The Gates of Hell."

Another benefit of having a golem as a partner is that everyone believes they can't think, that they only act on instructions given to them. I know Bernie's secret. None of the myths are true.

That night we staked out The Gates of Hell, a nightclub where it was rumored every craving might be satisfied for a price.

"Why do I have to wear the dress again?" Bernie tugged at the lacey neckline.

"Because we're undercover. No one thinks twice about a couple out on a date."

"But I'm a golem. Pharaohs wore dresses. I've seen the statues."

"It's called a shendyt and—"

I was cut off by a screech from overhead. A giant bird circled and landed nearby. It shimmered into a beautiful woman who entered the nightclub. After she was gone, Bernie walked over and picked up a single black feather.

Minutes later, the woman emerged with a finely dressed older man. He was nervous as she held his arm, leading him away. We followed. They turned down a nearby alley.

"I love a good dark alley," she said. "They have so much potential."

"I've never done this before." His hands shook as he placed one in the pocket of his coat.

"Just be quick. This isn't exactly painless for me."

He stopped, a gun in hand. "I didn't know this caused you any distress."

"Don't you worry. The money makes everything right for me."

She held out her hands, which he tied behind her back.

"No! Don't!" Her scream echoed off the alley walls.

He smiled as he leveled the pistol.

"Bernie, now," I said. We ran toward them.

The man pulled the trigger, and the sound echoed down the alley. She collapsed dramatically. He shot her again.

I pulled a foil blanket from my bag and threw it over the woman. There was a brilliant flash. The blanket deflated.

"Bernie, hold the edges down. Don't let anything out." I removed the gun from the man's hand. "And you, don't try to leave."

He nodded as the blanket started to rise, but the weight of my partner pinned it down. From beneath the blanket, the head of a large black bird poked out. It tried to peck Bernie, but he slapped it away. The bird shimmered and became the woman again, now barely contained by the blanket. She nearly broke free, but Bernie held tight.

"As I suspected. A phoenix. Every time she died, she was reborn anew, leaving behind a single black feather."

I called Krupke. He wasn't happy I had solved the case so quickly and without him. As they loaded our shooter and his victim into a squad car, I turned to Bernie.

"A brilliant but misguided scheme. Ra knows you can't have people shooting each other, even if it's an act. Innocents might get hurt or, worse, someone might get a taste for the real thing. On the bright side," I straightened my partner's collar, "if we get a few more feathers we can make you a nice boa to go with that dress."

"Shoot me now," Bernie said.

THREE WISHES

By James Scott Bell

Jonathan Milbank looked out at the ocean and the setting sun. A perfect L.A. time and place to do the Dutch. He'd just swim out as far as he could and drop to his death. That is, if his buoyancy didn't float him all the way to Catalina.

At thirty, Jonathan Milbank had let his once-athletic body go to pot. Literally. Seventy pounds overweight. Which brought complications.

He could see his shadow at high noon.

The underside of his chin looked like a stack of pancakes.

Then his girlfriend left him for a beach volleyball player—a tall, ripped, blond Adonis with whom Jonathan simply could not compete.

And so, as the sun began dropping into the sea that drizzly November evening, Jonathan took a step into the cold Pacific, and then stopped.

Do it now!

Back when he actually had some promise, Jonathan had learned this phrase from a motivational speaker.

Jonathan clenched his fists and took another step. "Do it n—oww!"

Something jabbed the bottom of his foot.

As the water ebbed, Jonathan saw it in the burnt-orange twilight—an odd-looking protuberance sticking out of the wet sand. He tried to bend over to grab the thing, but his stomach got in the way. So he got down on one knee and dug it out.

It was shaped like a teapot, only metallic and with all sorts of fancy designs on it.

Whoa! What if it was some sort of antique? His ex loved that kind of junk. Maybe he could give it to her—

He paused as something stirred in his ample gut. Hope! What an odd feeling to come over him then. But it was enough to save him, for he took the teapot back to his one-room apartment and set it on his coffee table.

He got a dishtowel and started rubbing off some of the sand. And then! Smoke billowed from the spout!

Jonathan yelped and dropped the pot on the floor. His shock expanded as the smoke morphed into the figure of a man. It had a beard and a turban and... and... hovered in the air!

"You called, Master?" the apparition said in a deep, melodious voice.

Jonathan couldn't speak. He could barely breathe.

"I am the genie of the lamp. Your wish is my command. *Three* wishes, to be exact."

I must be dreaming, Jonathan thought. Or insane. Yeah, that was it. Fruitcake time.

But what did it matter? He'd almost ended his own life an hour before. What did he have to lose by going along with this... whatever it was?

What if it *were* real? Could he—Jonathan Milbank—truly be reborn as a new, perfect self?

Do it now!

Jonathan placed his hand upon his corpulent flesh and rubbed. "Well, Mr. Genie. I would like six-pack abs right here."

The genie nodded. "It shall be so."

"And, um, I want to be thirty forever."

"It shall be done, Master. Do you have a third wish?"

"I... I think I'm going to hang onto that last one," Jonathan

Milbank said.

"I am sorry, Master, but did you say you do not desire to make a third wish at this time?"

"That's right. I've seen this movie. I need to keep one in my back pocket. So I'll take the first two, if you please."

The genie lifted his hand and, with a smile, snapped his fingers.

Jonathan waited a moment. He didn't feel a thing.

He lifted his shirt and looked at his stomach. It was the same size. But—

It was horribly discolored! Jonathan raced to the bathroom and looked in the mirror. The reflection showed a fat, dirty-faced man with strange markings on his corpulent abdomen. What? Were they... yes, they were! Tattoos!

A mix of images and script. But this was nuts! Tats of beer bottles in a carrying case, and beer cans bound together, and even reading backwards in the mirror he could make out the words—

Buy Corona!

Budweiser, King of Beers!

"What's going on here?" Jonathan shouted.

But there was no answer. The genie was gone.

Jonathan looked again at his face. Covered with grime.

But how?

He turned on the hot water and grabbed a bar of soap. He lathered up his face and rubbed all over with a wash cloth. He rinsed and looked at his face again.

No!

No change at all. He looked like a man who'd been living in a dumpster in an alley behind a slaughterhouse.

And his arms! They were covered with the same greasy, grimy dirt.

Wailing like a wounded dog, Jonathan rushed back to the lamp. He picked it up and rubbed it like a mad Boy Scout with two sticks.

With a puff of smoke the genie returned.

"Your wish is my command, Master."

"Are you kidding?" Jonathan said. "Look at me!"

"Do you like them?"

"Like what?"

"The six-pack abs right there on your stomach, and you wished to be dirty forever."

"Whoa, wait! I didn't ask for that!"

"No?"

"No!"

"Truly?"

"What is this?"

"I am so sorry, Master. But I am old and a bit hard of hearing."

"Can you hear me now?"

"Oh yes, Master."

"Then undo me! Right now!"

"As you wish," the genie said. He snapped his fingers.

And Jonathan Milbank disappeared from the face of the earth.

The genie returned to the lamp.

THE DOOMSDAY STONES

By Jebraun Clifford

My first assignment sounds simple enough. Contact the sentient life form on the ice planet Kalari Five, inform them of their sun's imminent supernova, and assist the United Planet Corp with their relocation.

The reality, however, is far more complicated.

"I thought Farons were qualified empaths." Lieutenant Jash, a Drik, folds four enormous arms across his well-muscled chest.

I smooth the bristling fur on my wrist. "We are." My breath creates frosty clouds in the pre-dawn dim. "But I'm having difficulty—"

"What Salah's saying is she can't do her job," mutters Sergeant Goss, one of the humans in our mission. "Knew we should've rounded up the aliens as soon as we landed. They'd be safe, and this whole sector could go kaboom with us far, far away. Job done."

I blink. "You realize *we're* the aliens?"

He cocks his head, staring pointedly at me. "Or we could strand 'em on this rock."

Frustration radiates from the other members of our expedition. I glance around the stony-faced humans, Driks, and the one Claspt. Her breathing mask hides her face, but no doubt she's scowling, too. Their resentment trickles down my spine and lodges in my two stomachs.

We've been here five standard weeks, and I've made no headway with the Kalari. They've accepted our presence, though I still cringe over my first bumbling attempts to communicate with them through thoughts. My introduction was the equivalent of *me nice, star bad.*

I explain again. "They're aware their sun will explode but also convinced they're not in danger. Every time I mention evacuating"—I motion toward the massive rock structure half a click away—"they take me to the Standing Stones. Again."

Lieutenant Jash shrugs. "If you can't persuade them to get on the transport in the next forty-eight hours, we'll forcibly remove them."

"But that's a violation of their self-determination!"

"How idealistic of you. But it's for their own safety." He presses an index finger against my sternum, nearly knocking me over. "Forty. Eight. Hours."

Goss smirks.

I trudge from our base camp to the Standing Stones and arrive just in time.

The Kalari, reminiscent of Terran emperor penguins, have already gathered for their morning ritual. A breeze ruffles their thick gray feathers, and I shiver despite my warm pelt. They hum, a low rumble sweeping through them. Every gaze fixes on the space between the two pillars.

The sky brightens, and the Kalari's collective anticipation ripples over me like warm, healing water. Such yearning. Such hope. A sliver of the ancient crimson star peeks over the horizon, slightly off-center through the two Standing Stones. In a moment, the sun is in the air, casting its wan light on the planet's pock-marked surface, and the hum ceases.

The Kalari leader, Flrrr, greets me with the image of her well-feathered nest tucked in the rocky cliff side.

"Srrr," she trills. *Welcome.* Her approximation of my name usually makes me smile, but not today.

I picture the sun's reflection on the ice-encrusted lake. *Star beautiful.* And it is. If only it wasn't going to explode, wiping them all out.

Her joy at my acknowledgement blooms in my chest.

Wait.

Could emotion convey the urgency? If I were frightened enough, would she understand? Heart pounding, I summon fear, imagining their sun going supernova.

She shakes her head and leads me closer to the Stones.

"Yes, I know." Impatience laces my thoughts and voice. "You've shown me this before."

She touches my temple with downy wingtips. In her mind, I witness the sun rising again and again between the Stones until its path blurs together in one continual arc across the sky. She shows me each Kalari's face, from Mrrr, the eldest, to Clrrr, the infant hatched yesterday. Each one confident. Jubilant. I stare into her whirling orange eyes, willing myself to discern her meaning, but all I take from the encounter is her absolute assurance of their safety and ours. What could they be waiting for?

Flrrr looks over my shoulder, quavering. I spin around. The Corp.

Goss approaches us. "We've got orders to evacuate." Soldiers fan out and herd the Kalari together.

I grab Goss's arm. "No!"

He shakes me off.

I sprint back to base camp and skid to a stop in front of Lieutenant Jash. "You said forty-eight hours."

"The star's destabilized. We need to leave. Now." The comm unit beeps, and he taps it. "Yes?"

"Goss here. Sir, the Kalari refuse to budge. How much force can we use?"

Lieutenant Jash glances sideways at me.

"Please," I whisper. "They're expecting something incredible. *Not* disaster."

He purses his lips, scanning the monitor, and sighs. "Stand down, Sergeant. I'll be right there." He points to me. "You have until sunrise."

When Lieutenant Jash and I get to the others, the Kalari have locked wings around the Stones. Nothing I communicate persuades them to move. The red sun passes overhead, Lieutenant Jash continually checking the readings. We wait through an anxious night.

Right before dawn, the Kalari begin to hum. The planet rumbles, and the ice on the lake cracks.

"Is this where we all die?" Goss hisses.

I focus on Flrrr, her head tipped back, her eyes closed. The hum grows louder. Louder. Wincing, I cover my tufted ears.

Again, the red sun makes an appearance, but now it's centered exactly between the two Standing Stones. The hum reaches a crescendo. A blinding flash sears the horizon. The air pulsates, and a wave of energy races toward us. It presses against me, through me, every molecule inside me lifting, renewing.

And the sun leaps into the sky, yellow, warm, young, bathing us with its golden radiance.

The Kalari squeak and dance around the Stones triumphantly.

Goss's mouth is open. "What happened?"

I exchange glances with Flrrr. That's what she tried to share with me.

"They knew the sun would regenerate." I can't stop the grin stretching across my face. I turn to Lieutenant Jash. "Sir, permission to cancel the evacuation?"

BITTEN

By Jessi L. Roberts

O nly someone with a death wish would risk trespassing on werewolf territory during the full moon, but Tari was as good as dead anyway.

Even though the night was cool, sweat ran down her brow as she forged through the dense underbrush. Her body fought a losing fight against the venom from the vamp bite. If she didn't get help soon, she and her unborn baby would die while their bodies lived on.

Most people said those bitten by vamps should kill themselves rather than turn into a bloodthirsty monster, but with the baby, that wasn't an option. She pushed deeper into the forest, her breath making clouds of mist that sparkled in the moonlight.

She shivered, not from the cold, but from the sickness running through her body. She had to find the werewolves before she turned. If her soul was gone, there wouldn't be any coming back.

She came to a clearing and strode into it, glad for the space. At least she could walk easily, and the moonlight was enough here.

Something pale moved in the trees.

Tari froze, her eyes locking with the wolf's. The creature watched her, its nose lifted, scenting her. It growled.

Tari dropped to her knees. "Please, I need you to bite me."

The wolf stared, then threw back its head and howled.

More wolves arrived, blending in with the darkness of the forest and moving like phantoms. There might have been five. She wasn't sure.

A massive dark gray wolf, his size dwarfing the rest of the group, padded toward her.

She looked up at him. The beast had to be bigger than a black bear.

Tari shook and bowed her head as the creature sniffed her, his warm breath on her neck. One bite, and he'd crush her skull.

"You've been bit by a vamp," he growled, his voice deep. "Why did you come here?"

She looked up into his golden eyes. "I'm pregnant. My child will die with me. I heard that you are immune, and I thought—" She couldn't bring herself to finish the sentence.

"We are immune to their bites because we're werewolves."

She held up her arm. "Please, bite me. Please. You're my only chance."

"You do realize this will turn you into a werewolf, correct?" He gazed up at the moon. "Not only that, you'll be a halfblood. The other packs will never accept you."

"Just do it," she said. Her whole body trembled from fear.

His massive head lowered. "Be glad our pack cares little for pack law. No other alpha would dare change a human, even when it was a matter of life and death." He seized her arm and bit down, his teeth sinking deep.

Tari cried out.

He released her and stepped back, waiting.

Tari's body blazed with an inner fire, one different from the painful sickness of the vamp bite. Her skin prickled and burned, the fire sinking deep into her bones. The baby fought within her as she doubled over.

Her teeth elongated, and bones rearranged themselves. Her cry of pain came out in an animalistic yelp. As her body grew, her clothes tore.

Finally, the changes stopped. She climbed to her feet, panting. The sickness had burned away. Instead, she was powerful, strong, and the night had become as bright as daylight. Her eyes widened as she stared down at paws that had been hands. Wild smells and sounds hit her from all directions. She ached to follow her new senses, to run and hunt.

The big wolf stood in front of her, still towering over her.

"Keep control of yourself," he growled. "That new instinct is powerful."

She felt her child move within, alive but changed like she was.

"Let's test out those legs," the dark wolf said. "Best thing for a new wolf is a good chase."

Tari raced with the pack, her mind buzzing with excitement, the smell of prey strong in her nose.

Then another scent hit her, one like stale blood. A vamp. Her hackles stood on end.

The other wolves turned to follow it, and Tari ran ahead of them, the thrill of the hunt surging through her. It was time for a rematch, and now she had a pack on her side.

The vamp wouldn't stand a chance.

THE CHOICE

By Kaitlyn Emery

My brain clung to every detail—sirens, flashing lights, muffled noises. Life wasn't supposed to end like this. I tried to deny what was happening, but my body knew what my mind refused to accept... My eyes grew heavy, and the world disappeared under my closing lids.

I felt like I blinked, and everything changed. It took a moment for my brain to register that I was sitting in a chair, no longer sprawled on the asphalt. All the pain from moments before had vanished.

"Next."

Next?

People of varying ages and ethnicity sat in chairs along the wall. Across the room, a plaque above the only door read *Second Chances.*

"Next." The door opened, and a bright-faced teen with fiery hair, a smattering of freckles, and bright green eyes peeked her head out. "Mr. Thompson, please step into my office."

"Me?"

The girl nodded and motioned for me to follow. As I entered the room, she moved to sit behind her desk, her smile disarming.

"Don't worry, Mr. Thompson. Your confusion is quite normal.

Please, have a seat."

It didn't seem optional. So I sat.

"Okay, so..." She shuffled through paperwork. "Your name is Peter Thompson, correct?"

My throat felt dry, so I nodded.

"Alrighty Mr. T, my name is Dani, and I've been assigned to discuss your placement."

"My what?"

Dani continued looking over her paperwork. "Your second chance placement. It appears you lived quite the..." She seemed to search for her next word. "...selfish life."

"I beg your pardon?"

"Well, that's a step in the right direction." She jotted something down. "Shows penance for wrong doing. Check!"

"Wait, what? I didn't mean—"

"Look, you died. I know that can be a shock, but we're a little backed up today and should get our tails moving, no pun intended," she said with a wink.

I didn't get the pun...

"So, what'll it be? Cat or dog?"

I blinked multiple times, trying to process her question. "I don't understand."

Dani let out a sigh, blowing fiery bangs off her forehead. "You've been admitted to the Second Chance Department. Upon death, you can go to one of three places. If you end up here, it's because you had a lifetime to make positive or negative choices and instead, you really did neither."

"Neutrality is a good thing, right?"

"Not in this case, Mr. T." Dani picked up a file and skimmed it with her eyes. "You were given a beautiful life to live with no disadvantages. There were no significant hardships to overcome, no poverty to struggle with, no physical limitations. You had all the advantages of race and physical appearance. You were given the opportunity to care for the people in your life, and you squandered that chance with your indifference and selfishness."

"Wait, so you're telling me I don't get credit for all the bad things I didn't do?"

"Life isn't just about not doing bad; it's about changing the lives around us."

"I did... stuff."

Dani blinked several times slowly. "Stuff?"

"Yes, stuff." My brain scrambled for something less lame sounding.

"What stuff?"

"My nephew got a nice check for his birthday every year... I don't yell at my maid... I watered my plants every day..." My list impressed me as little as it did Dani.

"Uh huh. As I was saying, you get another chance to bring love and happiness to others, but this time, you'll be given limitations. You'll be a house pet."

"Like reincarnation?"

"No, like a second chance. Your whole existence will be dependent on others—fed, bathed, taken outside, walked. You may be abandoned or mistreated—"

"Hang on! I could end up neglected or abused?"

"Unfortunately, that is a possibility every pet must face. Understand, your behavior and self-sacrificing nature is all you'll have to convince your owners to love you. So, dog or cat?"

My skin started to crawl. "That doesn't really seem fair, I mean, don't cats have nine lives or something?"

Dani smirked. "It doesn't work like that."

"Then how does it? What happens after I... come back?"

"If you're as selfish an animal as you were a human, you won't come back. You'll have used up your only chance." Her features softened. "But, if you bring love and joy into the life of someone on Earth, without the power of speech or the vast range of human emotions, you could have my job someday."

"You mean... you went back?"

Dani nodded slowly. "I came here homecoming night. The last thing I did was text my mom while driving to tell her she was ruining my life because my curfew was eleven."

Silence hung between us for a moment. "What did you choose?"

A fond smile spread across her face. "Cat, and I was lucky. I was sent as a kitten to a little girl who named me Angel. I lived with her for eighteen years. At her wedding, I wore a diamond collar and matching bow. She cried for days when my time was up."

A tear escaped the corner of Dani's eye, and for the first time in my life I felt the urge to comfort someone else. I placed a hand on her shoulder.

"Thank you," she said softly.

I waited a moment, then asked, "What do you think I should be?"

"People don't normally ask that."

"I didn't make good decisions in my life, clearly. Maybe I should trust someone else instead."

Dani smiled. "You know what, Mr. T, I think you're going to be okay." She quickly shuffled her paperwork and wrote in the notes. "I'm going to give you an advantage."

"An advantage?"

"Yes, I'll send you as a puppy. A cute little retriever. It doesn't guarantee anything, but it may help. Just remember, no matter what circumstances you find yourself in, you can always give love to those around you. Remember that, and you'll be okay."

THE MISFITS

By Samwise Graber

They call us the Misfits. They don't give us battle armor. Just what we can collect from the bodies of fallen friends and foes.

I tighten my grip on the overhead handhold as the dropship swings left.

Pop-pop-pop. The incessant thud of explosions around us warns that this is no training exercise.

"Contact in five minutes. Anyone still on this ship in six minutes will get a bullet in the back. Joren, are you planning on taking on the krax like that?"

I scowl at Sergeant Park and reach behind me for my red krax right-arm-piece. The piece has a tendency to fall off at unfortunate times.

I turn to my squadmate, Zara. "You ready for this?"

Zara glances at me, then looks away. Her hair's tied up in a messy bun today. Here in the Misfits, we don't have rules about how we look or dress, just strong suggestions. Zara is the only soldier on the base who refuses the suggestion of keeping short hair.

I admire that.

"You have anyone back home?" I ask her.

No answer. Zara never talks to me. Probably thinks I'm only friendly because I want something from her.

I don't blame her. Anyone with the ill-fortune to end up here is more than likely a criminal.

"Sixty seconds!" Park barks at us.

The ship rocks from the force of a nearby explosion.

We all reach one-handed for our helmets. I take one last survey of the surrounding faces, men I've lived alongside for months. I know the names of fewer than half of them.

By nightfall, more than half of us will be dead or dying.

I glance at Zara beside me.

Talk to me.

Maybe it's better to die as strangers, but I want to know where she came from. Does she have a family? And why did a woman as pretty as her end up here?

Helmets lock into place all around me, anxious faces replaced with expressionless masks of steel. Zara snaps on a red krax helmet with a skull on the forehead. I swear she picked it up on purpose to make up for her diminutive size.

My helmet is the last to lock into place. I reach behind for my gun.

The ramp slides open with a hiss and a rush of wind all around us. The ship takes a final dive then flattens out and hovers six feet above the ground.

"Go, go, go!"

I release my death grip on the overhead handle and lock my combat shield into place. Mine is the only shield the squad was able to pick up. The others are already pushing toward the ramp when I'm finished. I tail them to the foot of the ramp and jump. The impact sends a shock through my legs. I look through the mass of mismatched armor pieces for the red helmet. *There.* I take off after Zara.

Guns rattle out their staccato pulse over the crest of the hill in front of us. Park curses and waves us forward. I put on a burst of speed and reach the hilltop two steps behind Zara.

To the left, groups of Misfits are scattered along the ridge. Ahead, a wave of red advances through the brush.

Krax.

We're not meant to win, only slow them down until the regulars arrive.

Gunfire erupts around me. I catch up to Zara and push my shield arm in front of us both. A bullet pings off the metallic surface. The impact jolts through me.

The wave of red resolves into individual krax soldiers pushing toward the hilltop. I steady my gun on the side of my shield and open fire. One red figure falls.

Then the air is full of bullets whistling over our heads and clattering off my shield. I push Zara back from the crest. She shoves back against my chest and crouches to fire at the incoming soldiers.

We won't survive up here.

Instinct tells me to run. If she wants to die up here, that's her choice. I don't owe her anything.

Screw that. I crouch beside her and add my fire to hers.

More stuttering voices join the gunfire chorus. Colorful figures spill over the hilltop to my right.

Misfits.

The wave of red pauses then begins to recede. I shudder.

We're alive.

I stand along with Zara. My legs are trembling bits of wax that won't hold me properly. We're going to make it.

Thump-thump-thump.

The triple-thud is followed by a sharp whistle. The sound of our deaths. Three flame-trails speed through the air.

I dive into Zara, knocking us both to the ground, shield overtop of us.

BOOM.

The impact slams into me like a ton of bricks. My right arm-piece pops loose, sending my gun tumbling to the grass. Zara's skull-faced helmet rolls down the hillside, and I'm staring into a pair of blue eyes.

Zara mouths my name.

A line of fire traces its way up my left leg. Shrapnel from the blast. Our squad...

I can't think about that. We're lucky to be alive.

"Lie still," I tell her. "Help will come."

Zara's blue eyes never drift from my faceplate, as if she can see through it into my eyes.

"You saved me. Why?" she whispers.

"I just..." My voice trembles from the impact to my body. "I want to know you. To be your friend. I don't have anyone else."

Zara shakes her head. "We're going to die here, Joren. I don't have time for friends."

"No." I squeeze her steel-clad arm with my bare right hand. "The regulars are coming. We're going to be okay, and we're going to be friends. Just stay with me."

I don't care that my leg hurts like it's on fire, or if I'll ever be able to use it again. We're alive, and we're going to be okay.

Zara mouths that one word.

Okay.

GILDED FINALITY

By Brianna Tibbetts

The castle echoes with a nation's wailing.

I hear most of it with my soul; I share their sorrow. Worse still are the regent's theatrics, grating against my heart. I'm still in the throne room, taking gentle care of the body of the prince I raised. No one begrudges the fallen boy a moment with his nursemaid. Behind me, performing for a weeping audience, the new queen is declaring her anguish.

He wasn't even her son. My gut boils, promising a future eruption, but I can't pay it any attention now. My prince needs me. When he collapsed, the crown that once nestled atop his mountain of blond curls toppled and rolled away in the chaos.

As I finish the preparations to remove the sweet child I had raised, my eye catches on the glinting of the crown. I want to smash it. If he hadn't been royal, he'd be alive. The crown seems to agree—if I didn't know better, I'd say it was weeping.

Wait.

I squint at the ornate gold piece. It is weeping! The liquid bleeding from the precious metal is a sickening green hue. I whimper, the product of a tortured cry I won't let escape. I knew this was a scheme, but to see the proof of a curse with my own eyes is almost worse. How could anyone hate him so much?

I entrust my prince to the others, unable to tear my focus from the crown. I wrap my weathered hands in my skirts before I pick it up. The weight of it feels increased by the crime it aided in. The seeping evidence of the curse sizzles as it makes contact with my dress, wafting a stench like sulfur into my face. I'm forced to pause and breathe with care to avoid my supper fleeing my stomach.

I have no time to waste.

The blacksmith never leaves his forge, so I rush toward it, down the spiral staircases of the castle. Deeper and deeper into the bowels of stone where a brisk chill prevents most from venturing.

Thick gloves protect the blacksmith as I pass over the crown, his eyes careful not to stare at the gaping holes the curse has created in the folds of fabric swishing around my legs.

"It's cursed." I gesture to the forge, hope and retribution marrying in my chest. "Can the magic be re-forged?"

With a trained eye, the blacksmith examines the destructive headpiece. "Yes. It's still gold though—I'll have to lay it into steel to make it strong enough for you to use."

"I understand." It doesn't matter. The killer must not roam this castle for too long, basking in illicit victory.

The blacksmith tries to shoo me off so he can work, but I don't move. Instead I watch as the fires warp and eat away at the cursed gold. The glow of the forge flares, warming my blood while sending chills down my spine. The blacksmith's tools clink as he sets them out, preparing to mold an intricate design into a steel blade. Once cooled, the curse that took my prince will allow our kingdom to find justice.

Soon, the crown will no longer be a thief of innocent life. It will be a blade.

And I will sink it into the heart of the new queen.

EVERY DROP OF SOUL

By Lila Kims

Peter inhaled deeply, puncturing the quiet of the dark forest. One leg dangled from his perch on the tree while his gaze remained fixed on the small village at the bottom of the hill. The bark dug into his back, but he reclined against it as if it were the most luxurious couch.

He couldn't see her yet, but he would. Any moment now.

Tonight, the tribespeople were performing around an enormous fire in the center of their village. From this height he could clearly see the swell of flames, and around it the shadowy figures of dancing men and women and even children. Most were dressed in animal skins, but some wore little or no clothing. All were covered in markings of various colors from paints they had made themselves.

Peter scrunched up his face, then relaxed it with a bored sigh through his lips. It wasn't totally silent, he supposed. Loud singing and chanting, shouting and screeching, rose from the ritual into his ears, noises riding on the wind so faintly that they might have been coming from the top of the mountains beyond the woods. But they disgusted him.

Suddenly, and yet expectedly, he caught the firelit glint of a weapon out of the corner of his eye. A figure wove between huts toward the outskirts of the village. Her most precious possession—that wicked spear—was clutched in her hand.

Peter was glad she was coming *for* him to go *with* him, and not to kill him. At least, he hoped so. She always left her village looking like a warrior going out to hunt, with the sharp weapon and the painted face and all.

He clambered down the tree as nimbly as a squirrel and headed toward their regular meeting place, smiling into the dark as his stomach performed an excited somersault. Tonight was the night.

Peter made it his all-consuming duty to find and help individuals who were in need. Now he had the privilege of utterly *transforming* the life of a soul who simply did not fit. This beautiful girl in the depths of the darkest forest.

When he got to their meeting place, a glade out of the way of the village, he waited. It wasn't long before she melted into view, as stealthy and starry-eyed as a panther.

"Sounds as though your family and friends are having an exciting night," he reflected, glancing up at the winking stars.

Accustomed as she was to Peter's irony, she didn't comment on his use of the word "friends." That they were her family was inevitable, but if any of them had ever been a true friend to her, then she would not be a friend of his. The idea was rather appalling.

She walked up to him, eyes downcast. "I could not say goodbye," she whispered.

Peter examined the streaks of blue and red on her dark cheeks, noted the softness in her normally harsh eyes. "Yes, you are," he said with a crooked smile. "In your heart."

She took a deep breath, then lifted her head and squared her shoulders. Peter had been considering tilting her chin up with one gentle finger, but perhaps another time.

He slipped a hand into his pants pocket and curled his fingers around the tiny, corked vial. "Ready to go, darling?" His cheerful voice was louder now. He liked to imagine that all the simmering evils in the forest cowered at the sound of it.

"I do not know," she said, shoulders dipping once more. For the first time in the several months since they had met, he heard her voice crack.

Their first meeting had been unprecedented. Admittedly, she had taken him by surprise, holding him at spearpoint until he explained where he was from. And it took a very extraordinary remark indeed to fascinate the savagery right out of a huntress on the prowl.

Confused conversation had led to mutual intrigue with one another. Besides his light skin, blond hair, and blue eyes, she was entranced by his descriptions of the island and of his odd friends there, and he by her story: captured at a young age by a tamer, more nomadic tribe. Years of being taught a new perspective of life and being ingrained with a new set of morals. Then, recovery by her own when she was fifteen.

And with that recapture by her brutal family, the ruthless massacre of those she had come to love.

Peter still hadn't told her that he had most likely been the teacher of that more domesticated tribe, her second family, just as they had been a teacher to her. Years ago and in his spare time, of course.

"If you've changed your mind about going to my island, then I know you'll stay here. But one thing I've learned, darling"— Peter's mind fought back painful memories—"is that when you let go, you aren't letting go of your love. Only of those who will not or cannot return it."

She didn't smile, but the shine he had noted so many times during their many conversations seeped back into her eyes. She stretched out her hand toward him.

Peter took the vial from his pocket and gave it a playful shake, then handed it to her. She poured some of the sparkly golden dust into her brown palm, and he took some too. In moments they were ready to fly.

"Feel that tingling, Tiger girl?" Peter asked. "That's the magic settling deep inside you, saying hello to every drop of soul. Isn't it fantastic?"

"Let's fly," she urged, but there—*there* was the grin he had been waiting for.

He snatched her hand and beamed at the sky. "All right, then." His bare feet lifted from the ground as if with a soft kiss. "I'll let you know when we get to the second star!"

RUN

By Cathy Hinkle

The sharp stench of superheated metal burns your nose, making it difficult to breathe. Those scrubbers won't last much longer, not with all the smoke in the air. Metal framework moans, and flames roar from within the vault. If you're going to make it out of here, you've got to reach the ship before the abandoned facility collapses.

Don't think about the girder lying across the floor behind you. You need to run.

Your feet pound over the metal gridwork as you sprint away, vaulting over debris as it crashes into your path. The floor shifts violently, and you grunt as you catch your balance.

Keep moving. Get out.

Your pulse thunders in your ears over the screech of metal while your lungs fight for oxygen. Another explosion shakes the facility, hurling you against the riveted wall.

Push off. Run. Turn the corner.

There. Jess is still at the control panel. She shouts over her shoulder, "About time! It's taking everything I have to hold this place together! Did you find the temporal device?"

You seize her arm, spin her around.

"Easy, now—" She breaks off and squints past you. "Where's

Simon?"

"Gone."

"No—not Simon!" Her eyes widen, and she curses as she reaches for her pack.

"Not this time." You yank it out of her hand and throw it aside. "C'mon!"

"What d'you mean 'this time'?" she asks as the two of you race for the lift. "Did you find it?"

You manage to say, "Simon had it in his pack." That much is true.

"No! It's gone, too?"

"Move it, Jess!"

"That was the whole point of coming to this blasted outpost. If we don't bring it back—"

"Too late!"

Together, you dodge sparking, dangling wires, and when the power flickers off, you stagger through a nightmare of smoke tainted red by flashing emergency lights.

The lift's empty shaft is a gaping maw, and rubble blocks the stairwell. You and Jess toss chunks of metal and concrete aside.

She dashes tears and sweat from her eyes. "What happened?"

"I told him not to punch the button," you lie.

Your conscience screams to tell the truth just once, but you don't correct the lie you've already told a dozen times before. Don't think about Simon's protests, about your panic, about breaking protocol. You can't—not now—can't admit—

Her eyes open wide with horror, and for a split second, fear twists inside you. She knows you've mutilated the truth.

Then she asks, "He hit the button? He activated the device?"

Evade her questions. "Don't have time. Run!"

You grab her arm, jerk her back into motion, crawl through the hole into the fire-lit stairwell beyond. Then, Jess races beside you, her footsteps echoing out of sync with yours. The metal girders groan overhead as they begin to buckle. Again.

"Time? Time?" She gasps out the words, which stab you like shards of glass. "If Simon pushed that button—time is all we have! Of all the rotten luck, I'm stuck now? Couldn't it have been—"

The roar of the facility's collapse cuts her off. The world disappears as unmeasured metric tons of twisted metal plummet down, and the universe is nothing but pain.

The cacophony falls silent, and that silence swallows you whole.

You straighten, open your eyes, draw a breath.

Blink.

And once more, you're back in the long gallery. Once more, sweat trickles down Simon's face, leaving streaks like tears. His cracked glasses fog up. Behind you, fire crackles as the flames envelop the empty vault.

"Go," he grunts.

"Simon—"

"I'll hold it, as long as I can," he manages, jaw clenched with the effort of bracing the girder.

"I didn't mean—" You choke on the words, but you don't stop, don't try to change the future. You don't break the cycle, only duck past him. Again. Turn to face him. Again.

"You never have." For a second, his grimace splinters into a smile. "Get Jess out."

"I shouldn't've—"

"Just run!"

The weight is too much. With a percussive, sickening boom, the girder falls. You stagger backwards.

Simon's gone.

Again.

Turn away.

The sharp stench of superheated metal burns your nose, making it difficult to breathe; the scrubbers won't last much longer. If you're going to make it back to the ship before the facility collapses, you need to run.

Can't think about the girder.

Maybe this time...

Can't look back.

Just run.

SEEING IS BELIEVING

By Clarissa Ruth

"It'll be worth it. You'll see."

My brother, the perpetual optimist. "You're not the one puking over the side. Thanks to me, even the dragon probably wants this flight to be over."

Tad's chuckle was soft, but I could still hear it over the constant rush of air and the beat of the massive wings.

Whump, up. Down. *Whump.*

Oh no, not again.

Tad held my hair for me. Afterward, I groaned, shuddering as the headwind raced over my sweat. "I can't believe Mother paid one thousand silvers for this." She never gave up on me, although none of our doctors held out the slightest hope.

"From what I've heard, Hammu-Rapi may charge even more. But you're worth it." His hand made soft circles on my back, offsetting the hollow ache his words brought. Tad was always kind to me, but I didn't deserve any of it.

"Ha! Magicians and their tricks. If I choke on his smoke and die, please don't bury me in foreign dirt."

"Oh, Chrissy."

With a sigh, I lay forward, letting the lizard's body warm me. Nothing could help the icy ache in my heart. The daughter of a noble, but not eligible for marriage. No wonder Father shunned me. Even if someone could heal me, who would?

To distract myself, I traced little pieces of dragon armor. I counted one hundred sixteen before the beast coasted to a less-than-soft landing.

"Welcome to Ivirtir, passengers of the wing." The nasally voice spoke with a heavy accent. I was in a strange land now, like it or not.

"Do I have to move?" I muttered.

"Not if you want another ride," Tad said through an obvious smile.

"Mmmff. Fine." I gripped Tad's hand as he helped me to the ground. Though springy, the turf felt rock-solid to me, and released the glorious scent of grass. We found lodgings—insanely overpriced—and settled in.

We waited a fortnight, but it still seemed too soon when I stood before Chief Magician Hammu-Rapi.

His deep voice was soothing, but he smelled like a cacophony of herbs that made me want to sneeze. "My daughter," he began.

I'm not your daughter. Stop acting like you care.

"I'm thankful you came to Ivirtir. Here there is healing."

Tad jumped in. "A pleasure to be here, sir." He probably hoped to cut off my remark. As if.

"I'll believe it when I see you."

A slight breeze brushed my cheeks.

"You can stop waving your hand in front of my face." I sighed. "I can't see it."

He sniffed. "Sharp of wit and tongue, this one."

"Please, sir," Tad sounded worried. "It's just that she's been this way since birth—"

"Blind, or sarcastic?"

A sense of humor. That was something. Still, I willed Tad to not respond.

"Don't worry, young man," the magician continued. "Skeptics are my favorite patients. No, put your money away. The look on her face when we're done will be payment enough."

I had no comeback for that. *He's not just another greedy foreigner. What if he can heal me?* The ice in my heart started dripping, the drops turning into butterflies that tormented my gut. *Would he—even for me?*

He shuffled away. Jars clinked together.

When he returned, I crinkled my nose, and he laughed. "Here, I'll keep these herbs in my hand and put them behind my back. Now my other hand—pardon me, I must place it over your eyes. May I?"

I nodded.

His hand was meaty and warm, smelling of peppermint soap and sage. I didn't sense any sweat. My heart thumped harder, melting more ice. He didn't doubt himself.

Was his hand this warm at first? I kept my eyes closed, pressing them tight as the heat grew. *What's happening?*

My eyes began to tingle. I gasped.

"Chrissy?"

"Shh. Almost done."

When he withdrew, I stood trembling.

Tad put a hand on my shoulder but waited in silence.

The world was warm. Not to my touch, but through my eyes. Warm like fire, but without heat. Was this color?

"Open your eyes, daughter."

This time I didn't resent him calling me that. How could I, when he said it with such tenderness—so unlike Father? The ice was almost gone.

I opened my eyes to a riotous fanfare. *Colors... are all these colors? There are as many as there are sounds!* It was too much to process, but I couldn't bear to close my eyes again.

Finally I looked—looked!—down, trying to keep from reeling. Clenching my fists, I saw movement. I watched my hands come up, then rubbed my fingers and palms, combining touch with sight. Everyone said I have pale skin. *That's what the color "pale" looks like!*

I raised my gaze, looking for anything else pale. Instead I saw hands, these almost as dark as my familiar blackness. I grabbed one.

Tad gasped.

I brought the meaty palm to me. Peppermint and sage. I looked higher. Hammu-Rapi's face must be... there. Dark as his hands. But his eyes—oh, were those eyes?—were pale, with a center rich and sweet, like chocolate. Nothing could have prepared me for their depth, as if emotions echoed from them like my own voice from a deep well.

"I see you," I whispered. Father would accept me now, but I hardly cared.

From behind, Tad pounced on me in a fierce hug, sobs wrenching from his throat. "Oh, Chrissy!"

I staggered under his embrace, but I couldn't look away from those eyes. Though I'd never seen it before, I recognized compassion. Not for a girl who was blind, but for a girl who thought herself worthless. Now I saw myself through his eyes: I was a treasure. The ice was gone. Warmth spilled from my heart and leaked deep into my soul.

He smiled and cupped my cheek in his dark hand. "Welcome to a wider world, daughter."

"Thank you, Father."

ONE LAST TIME

By Robert Liparulo

The rider spotted the tollkeeper's cottage before he saw the gorge and the bridge beyond it. He rode closer, and a short man—as round as he was tall—shuffled out to greet him. He wore a mountain man's pelts and a pristine top hat. His silver-bristled face matched the area's rough terrain. One blue eye sparkled; the other was milky white. He lifted a shotgun.

Reining to a stop, the rider said, "Kevin don't appreciate that boom stick in his face."

"Y'r horse?" The man cackled and lowered the muzzle. "Universal feelin', I s'pose. Buyin' a toll?"

"Depends on the price." He dismounted.

"A pittance," the man said, "compared to the two-day's ride to the nearest natural crossing." He pushed his hat back and looked up to meet the rider's eyes. "Not to mention the extra benefit of using my bridge."

"I've heard it's... kinda magic."

The man frowned. "Don't know what, exactly, but it'll rid a man of... uh... unfavorable dispositions or grant 'im favorable ones. Whatever y'r fancy."

"How about *everything?*"

The tollkeeper nodded. "It can."

"How?" But in truth, the *how* didn't matter. Not as long as it worked. Not as long as he left his past behind.

The tollkeeper shrugged and waddled into the cabin, and the rider followed.

Inside, shadows draped over crowded shelves displaying flour, jerky, blankets, holsters, books, and much more. The rider paused to pick up a yo-yo with a boy's name carved into it. A *familiar* name. Other toys bore the same. He set it down beside an engraved pocket watch and a pair of distinctive wedding rings.

"So..." The tollkeeper sat behind a battered bar-top, "One toll plus Kevin?"

The rider walked to the bar. "You charge for horses?"

"I'd charge for their fleas if I had the patience to count 'em." He opened a heavy ledger on the dusty bar and scratched the rider's name across the bottom of a blank page.

The rider rocked back. "How do you know—?"

"Reputation precedes a man." The tollkeeper grinned a mouthful of crooked, stained teeth. "Gunslinger, bounty hunter, killer..."

"All of them had it comin'."

The tollkeeper bobbed his head. "But *sometin'* brought ya to my bridge."

The rider scowled. He wasn't about to explain to this geezer how every man he'd killed, from first to last, appeared to him every night, never speaking, except with their sad eyes. Or how they weren't the adults he'd gunned down, but the children they once were, before they turned nasty and greedy and deserving of a bullet. By now, he could expect a whole schoolhouse of boys crowding around him.

"Following my sister and her family," he said. " Shoulda come through about two—" Looking down at the ledger, he saw that his name had vanished from the page.

The tollkeeper slammed it shut. "Might've. Folks come here 'scaping one life, chasing another. No bitness a'mine."

"My nephew's toys are on your shelves, my brother-in-law's watch, their wedding rings."

"If'n so, no longer part of 'em."

"Why would they leave—"

"Ain't for me to tell people what ta change," the tollkeeper snapped. He sighed. "Now, that'll be ten dollar an' an item that represents what you's leavin' behind."

Something wasn't right. Why would Jacob leave his toys? The boy was eight, too young to want to grow up. And Lucy and Martin's wedding rings? They were happily married. But what could he do? He'd never killed without absolute proof of wrongdoing. If he traveled on and didn't find his sister, he could always come back.

He dropped a bill on the bar and stood a bullet upright beside it.

"Not your gun?" the tollkeeper asked.

"Ain't the gun that kills people."

The tollkeeper studied his face. "Right. Off ya go." He came around the bar and led the way back outside.

The rider took Kevin's reins and followed the tollkeeper toward the bridge. He was uneasy, sure that an injustice had befallen his sister and her family. But he hoped they'd simply got carried away with finding a new life back east; hoped his gut was wrong; hoped he'd never again face the boys who haunted him.

He wondered if temptation and doubt were part of abandoning an old life for a new one, if *something*—a darkness within or the Dark One himself—was trying to keep a gun in his hand and blood on his soul.

Keys rattled. The tollkeeper pulled open a gate and stepped aside.

The rider walked onto the planks of the long bridge, which spanned a bottomless chasm. Kevin's hooves clomped behind him. A quarter-way across, a breeze whipped his slicker and nearly stole his hat. And he felt it: something changing within him, a calmness, a release of the tension he had always felt. He knew that once he crossed, there was no coming back. He wouldn't want to. He couldn't. He released Kevin's reins and turned around.

Behind the closed gate, the tollkeeper gave him a deep frown. His eyes became huge marbles. He turned and ran.

The rider drew his weapon, fired. The tollkeeper went down, kicking up a plume of dirt and sending the top hat sailing. Kevin galloped off for the far side. The rider plugged the downed man twice more, then continued toward his new life. By the time he was halfway across the bridge, he'd lost the rage that had killed the tollkeeper. When he stepped off the planks onto the rocky ground on the other side, he looked back. A fiery sunset silhouetted the cabin—and what looked like a short, fat man.

The rider was not surprised. Something about the wonder of this place. He felt no concern, no anger. He waved at the dark figure, which waved back.

The rider walked off to find Kevin. As he did, he unbuckled his gun belt and let it fall. He felt certain that tonight he would not see any ghost-boys. Not tonight or ever again.

UNNATURAL 20

By Andrew Swearingen

The barbarian exploded from the folding table, launching dice, game pieces, and potato chips in every direction.

Tony, Piper, and Bart dove to the carpet for cover.

"What did you do?!" Piper screamed at Tony.

"What did *I* do?!?" Tony army crawled away from the disaster.

"Yeah, you butthead. *You* rolled!"

"Are we gonna die?" Bart squeaked from under his chair.

The barbarian groaned, pushed himself up from the soda-drenched carpet, and wrapped his fingers around the hilt of his sword.

"Who dares attempt to capture Anton the Great?!" The barbarian stood to his full height, shaking dark matted hair out of his face.

Tony and Piper scooted further away, suddenly wishing for chairs of their own.

"I swear by my ancestors' souls, whoever has attempted my capture shall pay with their... blood!" Anton unsheathed his sword, swung it in a wild arc, and stabbed at the remains of the table. His bloodshot eyes surveyed the room and evaluated the trio of tweens.

"What kind of coven is this? Are you magic-wielding halflings?"

Tony gulped, hopped to his feet, and held up his hands. "Great Anton... the Great. We brought you here through our magic, for we are... fans of your orc killing."

Anton rubbed his stubbly chin and adjusted the green amulet strapped to his wrist.

Piper stepped forward. "Yes. We *are* magical. And we offer you the hospitality of our humble dwelling." She gestured to Bart, speaking through gritted teeth. "Why don't you get our honored guest some refreshment?"

Bart shuffled on his knees, picked up a crushed bag of Doritos, and offered them to Anton.

The barbarian glowered, pointing his sword at Bart's bellybutton. "If this is an attempt to poison me, you will not live to tell of it."

In a show of quick thinking that surprised both Tony and Piper, Bart shoveled a fistful of broken chips into his mouth and chewed vigorously. "Not poisoned." Orange flecks spewed from his lips.

Anton slowly stuck a meaty hand into the bag, retrieved a small sample of the snack, and chomped on it. Confused elation crossed his face.

"Ha!" Anton seized the bag from Bart. "I like these! I shall have more!"

The barbarian plopped his hulking frame down on a beanbag chair. "Fetch me something to drink, for my thirst is great."

Piper prodded Bart along. "Keep him happy," she said as she and Tony stepped aside into the stairwell.

"Well, this is a great mess you've gotten us into." Piper glared at Tony.

"Me??" Tony shook broken chips out of his curly hair.

"Anton the Great? That's your character. You didn't recognize his sword, the Decapitator Express?"

Tony sat on the bottom step and peered through the stair railing at the barbarian, who sat licking Dorito dust from his fingers. "He's even got the scar on his chest from fighting that three-headed pig-bear." Tony smiled giddily. "Just like in the game."

"Stop fanboying," Piper said. "How did this happen?"

Tony bit his lip. "The thing on his wrist! It's the relocation amulet. We were trying to pass the Mudwood Lagoon, and I rolled to use the amulet."

"You're right." Piper punched Tony in the shoulder. "This *is* your fault. You could have made up nonsense words for the incantation, but *noooo*. You had to use actual Druidic."

Anton the Great belched heartily as he guzzled Mountain Dew.

"Did you write some way to reverse the spell?"

"Well yeah, there's a reverse incantation." Tony rubbed his shoulder. "But there's no way to know if it would work."

"Of course it'll work. That amulet brought him here in the first place. Use that Druidic mumbo-jumbo to send him back."

"Whoa." Tony held up his hands. "Could we look at the bright side? We have our own barbarian! This is great!"

"'Great?'" Piper sneered.

"Sure. He could help us. He could beat up Kyle Crowl for us."

"Are you stupid? He would disembowel Kyle Crowl."

"You say that like it's a bad thing."

Piper rolled her eyes. "I'd think you would have a little more hesitation about hacking up our classmates."

"MORE DORITOS!!!" bellowed Anton the Great.

Piper sighed, crossing her arms. "Dude, you realize he isn't a good person, right? He's the one who starts brawls in every tavern and robs random strangers."

"Hey!" Tony pointed at Piper. "We all said that was faithful to the character. Besides, I always gave some of that stolen gold to you and Bart."

Bart offered Anton the Great a bag of dried banana chips his mother had sent with him.

"Yeah," Piper said. "And it was hilarious. But that was the campaign. Here? Less funny. We can't control him. You think we'll be able to buy him off with Doritos once he figures out there's a world beyond this basement? A world where he has access to booze?"

Tony peered through the railings. The barbarian held Bart by the shirt—much like Kyle Crowl often did to Tony—and spat half-chewed banana chips in Bart's face.

Tony hung his head. "He's just another bully, isn't he?"

Piper put her hand on Tony's shoulder. "Yup. A bully with a broadsword."

Tony nodded, stood up, and stepped out of the stairwell.

"Anton the Great!" he yelled. "Your respite here is over. It is time to return to your quest."

The barbarian grunted. "Fetch me more food, little wizard. I have not yet satisfied my hunger."

Tony narrowed his eyes. "You are no longer welcome in this realm. Begone!"

Anton the Great shoved Bart to the ground and stood, reaching for his sword.

Tony raised his arms. *"SÊM-ah-NÙM, OMË-om-SÅÅL!"*

The amulet gleamed. A flash of emerald lightning filled the room, and Anton the Great vanished.

Piper helped Bart to his feet. The three friends surveyed the damage from their encounter. Tony picked up the tiny pewter figure of Anton the Great.

"Tony," Piper said, "your character is truly a butthead."

Tony nodded.

Bart peeled a soggy banana chip off his cheek. "So... Mario Kart?"

DUNE BUGGY DASH

By Katie Robles

When Dad took him out of school and drove two hours south to his favorite state park, Carl thought it was an early birthday present. When Dad strapped five-gallon jugs of water into the extra passenger seats of the rented dune buggy, Carl wasn't sure what to think.

"Hey, mister," said the tanned woman holding the rental agreement. "You got enough to drink?"

She looked pointedly from the water jugs to the two dozen large bottles of cola on the floor in the back. Dad ignored her and slid a cardboard box in next to the cola before climbing into the driver's seat. He had that focused make-the-flight look he got at airports.

"You know we close in an hour," said the woman.

Dad put the buggy in gear, and Carl gave the woman a nervous wave and a smile. The buggy rumbled, then pulled away from the irrigated trees of the visitor center and turned to follow the trail through the desiccated forest.

Despite Dad's odd behavior, Carl smiled when they reached a gigantic bowl of cracked dirt littered here and there with old docks and dry canoes. He knew this place. Grandpa had spent his childhood fishing here, and Dad had gone four wheeling in the muddy lake bed as a teenager. Now there were dune buggies.

Carl let out a whoop as Dad planted his foot on the accelerator, but when they reached the far shore, Dad turned off the established trail and aimed the buggy at the horizon.

"Dad?"

Dad's eyes had circles under them. "Open the glovebox."

Carl flicked the latch up. Inside the glovebox were photographs. Just photographs. The first looked like a flower with lollipop petals. It had the clear center and fuzzy background typical of microscope pictures. Carl flipped to the next one.

"Oh, Dad, gross!" Carl squeezed his eyes shut, but the image of the bad case of pink eye was still there. "Just because you're used to this doesn't mean I am."

Dad never brought home photos from the hospital pathology lab; it violated patient privacy. Carl was used to hearing about death and disease, but a photograph was so much more disgusting than the medical terms Dad normally used to describe his work.

"It's not pink eye," said Dad.

Carl made a face and looked again. The white of the eye was completely pink, and tiny balls of yellow gunk had formed at the base of the lashes.

"Her diagnosis was pneumonia, but when I opened up her lungs, they were red," said Dad, adjusting his grip on the wheel. "Not healthy blood-red, but a fuzzy, slimy red."

Carl held up the microscope flower picture. "And this?"

"That's a fungus spore. Similar to Aspergillus, but this one's different."

The way Dad said "different" made the hair on Carl's neck stand up. "How?"

"Six hours, Carl. It killed her in six hours."

Dad pressed the gas down harder, and the buggy's oversized wheels bumped across the open ground. The water in the jugs sloshed.

"I don't understand."

"We breathe in fungus spores all the time, especially when the weather's been wet," said Dad, squinting against the sun as the buggy bumped onward.

The weather had been record-breaking wet for years. The rain that used to fill the lake had shifted north to their town.

"If your immune system is strong, it should be no big deal. This woman was healthy, had just retired..." Dad's voice faded, but Carl heard him whisper, "Six hours."

Next in the stack was a satellite photo. Carl recognized the north part of town. Little, red dots were scattered over it: seven at the nursing home, three on homes in a neighborhood, two in a shopping center. The photo was dated three days ago.

"This woman lived in that neighborhood." Dad slowed through a patch of sand. "The nursing home thought they had a flu outbreak."

"These dots are..."

Dad nodded.

Carl stuffed the photos back into the glove box and slammed it closed. He tucked his hands under his thighs and let Dad's words sink in. His brain was making connections he didn't like. He leaned over the seat and reached for the box Dad had packed in the back. When he opened it, he wasn't surprised to see jars of peanut butter and boxes of raisins. Food for days.

"Dad, you have to warn people."

"I did." Anger made Dad's voice tremble, his knuckles white on the steering wheel, but then it softened. "I *tried*. I sent evidence to the mayor, the news station, the hospital, the schools, radio stations. They didn't want to cause a panic."

"But Dad—"

"Look at the last photo."

Carl slid it from the glove box. It was another satellite photo, this time of the whole town. Carl could only identify the largest buildings: his high school, the mall, the hospital where Dad worked. There were dozens of dots on the map, clustered near the north and thinning as they spread across town to the south, like someone had dropped a red paint bomb on the dead woman's neighborhood. The date on the photo was today.

"Can I call my friends?"

Dad nodded.

"If there's an... an outbreak..." Carl hesitated. The whole thing sounded like a Sci Fi movie, not a Tuesday afternoon. "Will the desert protect us?"

"I hope so. Fungi need moisture, so the desert will be a good barrier. We'll warn the authorities on the other side."

The desert was huge. To cross it they would need... He looked back at the cola bottles, at the way the dark liquid clung to the plastic. It wasn't soda: it was gasoline. Clever Dad.

Carl reached for his phone.

If he hurried, maybe some people still had a chance.

ORDAINED

By Tracey Dyck

A leida's hands trembled as she picked up the single gray satchel carrying her belongings, and then secured her wand in its straps around her leg.

It wasn't supposed to happen like this… not so soon.

Late-afternoon sun poured through her cottage's skylight and painted the floorboards golden. The house seemed too large now, too empty, all the furnishings cleared out.

Aleida snapped her fairy wings open and stepped outside. Time to go.

The door closed behind her with a thud of finality. If she spared even one backward glance, she knew she'd weep in earnest. So she took off flying toward the Pocket's central glen, following the path beneath the twisted limbs of coil-trees.

When she touched down, breathless and tear-choked in the grassy glen, fairies of all ages already filled the expanse. In the middle, a dozen of them stood alone.

"Come forward, Aleida." One of the dozen, Orcallon, beckoned. His wings swept to his feet in gleaming ebony folds.

Aleida waded through the silent gathering and bowed to the Fifth Order of the Pocket.

"The hour has come for your ordination." Orcallon's deep

voice belied his many centuries. "The kingdom of Iror requires a new fairy steward to protect its boundaries, prosper its people, and advise its rulers. Do you, Aleida, swear to do so?"

Aleida's wings wrapped around her shoulders like a cloak, their translucence painting her skin in soft green hues. They would never have the chance to mature—to grow opaque and silky like a butterfly's wings. Everything was changing. It was too much. Too soon.

I'm not ready, her heart whispered.

Up. You have a job to do. That's what Steward Mina would say, if she were still alive. Though sharp-tongued, she was the closest thing to a mother Aleida had known. And now she was gone, crushed in a landslide before training an apprentice to take her place.

Orcallon's question was only a formality. Aleida locked her shaking knees. "In the footsteps of Steward Wilhelmina before me, I swear to give my kingdom my protection, my loyalty, and my wisdom." It's what Mina would have expected, though the words grated against her throat. What wisdom did she possess? She was still a child by fairy standards, barely over thirty.

"Then, by the magic in the bones of the Earth, I, Orcallon, Head of the Fifth Order, strip you of your wings." He extended his wand. Pure white mist shot forth and surrounded Aleida, obscuring the glen from view.

Nothing could've braced her for the agony that bloomed deep within her muscles—that ripped at her wings like a hurricane tearing a tree out by its roots.

Aleida screamed and hit her knees.

All at once, the mist vanished, and her sight cleared. Members of the Order pulled her to her feet. She wobbled, exposed and unbalanced without the extra weight on her back.

"And now," Orcallon boomed, "wingless you shall walk in the

land of humans. The Pocket ordains you Steward of Iror. You shall bear this title for the rest of your days. May Aon's face smile upon you."

As one, the fairies of the Order raised their wands. Twelve streams of mist swirled around Aleida's ankles, setting her skin tingling.

In an instant, the glen's golden hues whirled away, and Aleida lurched on new ground, rocky beneath her bare feet. Gone was the Pocket. In its place rose proud, green mountains, the valleys below swathed in evening shadow. Iror.

Shoulders throbbing and legs unsteady, she began the familiar trek down the mountainside to Mina's house. How many summers had Aleida spent here, clinging to Mina's shadow? Though the route was one she'd taken many times, emptiness loomed behind her. This time, there was no way back.

This human world was home now.

Why did they choose me? Why?

By the time she reached the ravine cloven into the foot of the mountain, night had fallen. But she knew the uneven path by heart—could almost hear Mina calling from up ahead to hurry. Moonlight illuminated the mouth of a cave to the left, where the hulking shapes of Mina's two dragons lay. One whined in its sleep.

Poor things. They must miss her, too. Aleida swallowed. *I suppose... they're mine now.*

On the right, she found Mina's house carved into the ravine's side. The door was unlocked, the room beyond cold and dark. Too exhausted to conjure a light, Aleida fumbled for the candles kept just inside the doorway and lit one. Its feeble glow illuminated the barest hints of overflowing bookshelves and a neatly made bed. Everything just as Mina always left it. Aleida dropped her satchel to the floor.

A light sparked in the corner of the room. It bobbed through the air until it hovered in front of her nose—a pebble, maybe the size of her thumb, glowing as if doused in sunlight.

"Those blasted brambleheads say I should choose an apprentice," the rock said.

Mina's voice! But how—

"I can't just yet. The one I want is too young. But if the mantle of stewardship should fall to her before her time, she must hear this message." The snappish voice softened. "Aleida, if you're hearing this, it's because I never got to tell you myself. You were always meant to be my apprentice. I know the Order chose you for a reason. Serve your kingdom well, my dear. They will have need of you."

The voice, along with the light, faded. The pebble clattered to the floor.

Aleida sank down with it. She clutched the rock to her heart, tears welling once again. The Order's decision she did not understand. But Mina had wanted her. Planned for her.

Someday, maybe this stone house and these lofty mountain peaks would feel like home.

IF THESE WALLS COULD TALK

By J. L. Knight

T*hey were arguing again. He could hear their voices rising, drowning out the sound of Johnny Carson on the TV. He pulled the covers over his head and tried to ignore them.*

"Ugh, this stupid cabinet. I can never get this door open," she said.

Downstairs, something smashed. His mother's voice was becoming shrill and hysterical. His father's was a low, threatening rumble, hard to make out the words. Another crash, then a sharp crack. Abruptly, the shouting stopped. Slaps and thuds mingled with the laughter from the TV. He recognized the sound of fists hitting flesh.

"Mom! Can you come up here and help me, please? The door is stuck again!"

An unnatural silence fell over the house. Usually their fights ended with his mother quietly sobbing and cursing his father, but tonight there was nothing. He listened intently. Johnny was doing his Carnac the Magnificent routine. He was starting to relax when he heard his father's slow, heavy footsteps on the stairs.

"Why did we even buy this stupid house? I liked our old house better."

"Oh, hush. We'll have your father look at it when he gets home."

"He already did. It still sticks."

His heart began to pound. He'd been hoping his father would forget about him up here in his room. The footsteps were getting closer. He slipped out from under the blankets and crept to the little built-in cabinets in the wall under the windows. Noiselessly, he opened one of the doors and crawled inside, then closed the door behind him. There was a knob on the inside as well, and he clutched it tightly, his knuckles white.

"Well, maybe you should find someplace else to keep your things."

"This room is tiny. There is nowhere else."

"Oof. You're right, this door is really jammed shut. Come over and help me pull."

His father entered his room, breathing heavily. Roared his name. Began tearing the room apart, looking for him. It didn't take long before his father got to his hiding spot. He clung desperately to the knob, crying as his father pulled from the other side. He was no match for his father's strength, even when stinking drunk. He knew he was making it worse. He could hear how angry his father was on the other side of the door. The knob was slipping from his aching fingers...

"There! Finally!"

"Yeah, for now. It'll just get stuck again. I hate this house."

"Will you please just try to make the best of it? You know we had to move for Dad's job. We all have adjustments to make. I'll call you when dinner's ready."

She scowled at her mother's departing back. Behind her, she thought she heard a tiny sound, like a child's stifled sob. She turned around. The cabinet door swung slowly closed again, the latch engaging with a soft click.

CORRUPTION'S KISS

By Margaret Graber

There are three rules for being an assassin. Don't hesitate. Don't question. Don't feel.

Emotions get you in trouble, and the pain of the past is a distraction.

I glide through the crowd, sipping my champagne and smiling at everyone who meets my eye. I know how to act like just another beautiful woman. I used to be one, after all. No one expects beautiful women to have guns strapped to their thighs and knives between their shoulder blades underneath cocktail dresses.

I check my watch for the time. 23:30.

Thirty minutes.

I glance around. The room is enormous in size, but it doesn't feel big with everyone packed in like bullets in a magazine. It's so hot it makes me regret deciding to wear a floor-length dress, though that's just part of the job.

I make my way toward the restrooms, but then I catch a glimpse of sparkling-green eyes in the crowd. My composure wavers. I don't want to remember.

A sweet voice giggling and a soft, smiling face.

Lily.

I block the memories with a mental wall and step into the restroom. After scanning to confirm I'm the only inhabitant, I jam the doorstop underneath the door frame. It won't hold against much, but it will be a crude alarm if anyone disturbs me.

I move into a stall and shut the door, then climb onto the toilet. I take a decorative hairpin from my hair and flip it around, revealing the screwdriver on the other end. There's an air-vent grate on the ceiling above the stall, which I quietly unscrew. Once it's off, I hoist myself into the vent, then secure the grate behind me. Following the directions in my head, I crawl through the steel ductwork.

It takes five minutes to reach the right grate. According to their plans, the grate should lead to an empty bedroom. I peer through the slats and see slivers of a bed.

Good.

I unscrew the grate, then drop out of the vent and land softly on the bed. It takes a split second for me to survey the room.

Clear.

I stride over to lock the door, then cross the room to the closet and reach inside to grab the suitcase they said would be waiting for me. Inside it are black boots and a black suit with gloves. I remove my dress and heels and slip into the outfit, then switch my white silk gloves for the black leather ones. A compartment in the bottom of one of my pumps holds a small key, which I use to unlock the case hidden at the bottom of the suitcase.

Inside are the pieces of my sniper rifle. I assemble it in twenty-three seconds, and then it lies before me, a sleek black monster with its name engraved on the side: Corruption's Kiss.

I don't know why the name nauseates me. Maybe it's because I know how much everyone else should be afraid of it. Of me.

Don't hesitate. Don't question. Don't feel.

I sling the rifle across my back.

The air is so cold it bites into my skin as I step through the room's french doors onto the balcony. My adrenaline begins to climb in anticipation, the same rush as always. But this is just another shot, and I know the drill.

Get in. Get out. Target eliminated.

A small shiver creeps up my spine.

They told me it was natural to think about the targets, that I just have to remember the rules. I can't spare a thought. Why would I, anyway? I, of all people, have learned how fleeting life is. Here one heartbeat, gone the next.

I push aside those thoughts, then reach for my thigh holster and sweep out my grapple gun. I shoot a hook up above me onto the roof. It holds, and I pull myself up the side of the building to the top. I can see almost all of the city from up here.

I knew someone who would have loved this view.

No, I tell myself. *That doesn't matter.*

Sinking down to the rooftop onto my stomach, I aim my rifle's scope towards a tall skyscraper, then check my watch. 23:58. The remaining countdown begins as I zoom in on the sixth level, three windows from the left. They told me the target would be wearing violet and have red hair. That's all I know. That's all I *need* to know to make the shot.

One minute, thirty seconds.

I wait for my target to appear. There's movement, and a black-haired woman enters the room, laughing about something. I ignore her. The abrasive gravel of the rooftop digs into my hip. I ignore that, too.

One minute, ten seconds.

There's a flash of red hair as someone walks in after the woman. It's a girl. My heartbeat halts, though my finger remains on the trigger.

She's a child. She's just about the same age as Lily was.

Fifty seconds.

Instead of the rush assuring me this mission will be a success, a strange ache squeezes my heart.

Thirty seconds.

I see the two embracing like Lily and I used to embrace.

Ten seconds.

They told me my daughter's death was a terrorist attack. Will they tell the black-haired woman the same thing?

Zero seconds.

I pull the trigger.

The window shatters, and the bullet finds my target.

It hits the security camera on the wall.

The girl and her mother duck to the ground just as another shot fires over them, coming from another rooftop.

Don't hesitate. Don't question. Don't feel.

I lift my chin and let out a breath, releasing an aching weight I didn't know I'd been carrying.

I'll break every rule they give me.

PROTEUS

By Kerry Nietz

Proteus's hue was an anomaly, a seeming mockery of its parent, Neptune. *That* planet—all science officer Jackal could see from his position in the flight deck of reconnaissance ship *Jambiya*—was solid blue. No pinks like its circling satellite. No browns or greens like Earth. Only blue.

"Why are we here again?" ship pilot Serif asked.

Jackal shot him a look. "You didn't forget. I don't—"

Serif waved him off. "Yeah. Accident inspection and ore recovery. I know." He pointed a thumb at the window. "It's oppressive, Neptune. Too large. Too blue."

"That isn't our worry. Only finding the lost ship and recovering its ore." Jackal squinted at his screen's topography of the moon. Proteus was an ugly place. Not large enough to have formed a perfect sphere, but almost. A skewed, heavily-cratered polyhedron. "Missed it by that much."

"Missed what?" Serif looked his way.

"Nothing." Jackal felt a tickle of apprehension. "Not seeing anything here. You?"

"Nope. No distress signals. No location pulses. Nothing." Serif touched a couple green spots on his screen's surface. "Where could it be?"

Jackal shook his head. "Nothing in the visual band either. Like it vanished."

"Exploded?"

"Should be a debris field, right? No sign of that." His screen highlighted various locations on the moon's surface. "There are metal markers, but Proteus has graxin reserves. Always messes with orbital scans."

"I have the ship's last known location."

"Good. Then that's where we should land."

Two hours later, they rested atop a generally level plain amidst a panorama of crags and mountains. Uncertain dangers. Proteus's pinkness was subtle here. Barely perceivable. Hidden.

Further scans showed little trace of the ship, or its crew, aside from a single, anomalous reading. They suited up to investigate using the ship's two-seated rover.

"Where to?" Serif said as they rumbled onto the surface.

Jackal studied the rover's scans. "Still showing non-ferrous metals to the west." He pointed left. "That way."

Serif gunned the engine, and they were underway. They skirted massive craters and jutting hills. Neptune ruled the sky. Minutes passed.

Serif broke the silence. "There are mining bots here somewhere, right? Might be picking those up."

"Maybe. The largest is about the size of the rover. An XV unit. Four meters square, treaded. Has a collection basket in front, round head on top. Here, I'll show you." Jackal produced an image of the XV on his screen.

Serif studied the image, then pointed to the robot's head. "Is that a face on there?"

Jackal snorted. "Yeah, engineering does that sort of thing. Paints faces to make them seem human." He shook his head. "Silly."

Serif nodded. "What about the others?"

"Harvester drones. They're smaller." He brought up a drone image.

"Like fat spiders."

Jackal chuckled. "With an appetite for minerals scraped from crushed rocks."

"How do they do that?"

Jackal couldn't help himself. "Guess they have sharp teeth."

"Great." Serif looked toward the horizon. "I'll keep my eyes open."

Thirty minutes later, they reached the source of the readings. It was... unexpected.

A five-meter-high pyramid, as aesthetically imperfect as the moon it stood upon, and seemingly made from whatever materials were available. Poles jutted out at odd angles or stopped too soon. Metal plating and other flat items formed the outer surface.

Serif stopped the rover ten meters away. "Close enough? Don't want to mess with your analysis."

"It's fine," is all Jackal could manage. He got out and Serif followed. Jackal carried a handheld com unit, tied to the rover's scanning array. As they approached the structure, he studied its many intriguing and seemingly contradictory results. "The materials came from our lost ship. In fact, I think they *were* the ship." He indicated the pyramid's top. "Except whatever that is up there."

The pinnacle was composed of ten glowing spheres arranged in the shape of a smaller pyramid. Their precise chemical composition was hard to nail down. At times, they didn't even appear solid.

"Trans-dimensional?" Jackal muttered. "Possibly extrasolar."

"What?' Serif laid a gloved hand against the side of the pyramid. "Feels normal to me."

"No. The top. The shiny spheres."

Serif patted his helmet, then searched the horizon in all directions. "Who did it? Who built this?" He looked at Jackal.

"The crew members? What were their names? Longstring and Solstice?"

"I don't..." Jackal noticed something on the structure and walked closer. The edges of every part, every post and plating, showed a similar swirled pattern of scrapes. "Look at these." He pointed."That's not from being dragged over the surface. Looks more like machine handling." He examined a place where a plate attached to a support pole. "And how is this put together? Looks welded here, but up here..." He pointed at a higher spot. "It's glued." He stepped to the right, squatted. "And down here, bound together with string." His trepidation returned. "At least, I *think* that's string..."

"Using whatever they had. Reusing and repurposing."

Jackal's stomach lurched, and he gasped for air. Sweat stung his eyes. "Whatever happened here wasn't good. And I think those spheres are the cause." He took a step toward the rover. "We need to get back. Report this."

His comm unit chirped, then the screen exploded with new readings. Metallic objects. Motion. He looked to the horizon and saw rolling, metal spheres. Harvesters. They encircled the men and the rover within seconds.

"Run!"

The XV robot—the one with the face—rolled into view. As the harvesters closed in, the XV trundled toward them, a mechanical arm raised.

Serif made a retching sound.

"Serif?"

Another cough. "We know where one of the men went, Jackal. Look at its face!"

The robot's head wore a mask now. The front of a skull. Glued into place.

"He got recycled!"

Jackal tore his vision away. Focused on the rover. On reaching safety.

A harvester smashed into him, pushing him to the ground. He realized it then. In Neptune's shadow, Proteus wasn't pink at all.

It was red.

TO FIND A THIEF

By E. A. West

"You wanted to see me?" I tried not to fidget, but anxiety hit every time I got called into the restaurant's office.

"Where's the silverware?" Mr. Jones glared at me, his already small eyes squinted.

"What silverware?" I smoothed the front of my uniform, an ankle-length black dress with a lace-edged white apron. I hated the thing but was grateful for the busgirl job.

"The silverware you've been taking off the tables."

"In the kitchen, I assume. That's where I always put it, anyway."

"Nice try, but I know you've been stealing some of it." He rubbed his fleshy face. "This is what I get for hiring a petty thief."

"Former thief." I fought to keep my temper under control. I'd shoplifted once when I couldn't afford groceries and gotten caught. Even though I'd paid for my crime, it still haunted me. "I don't steal anymore."

"And yet the silverware is still missing. The same silverware you clear off the tables."

"Every fork, spoon, and knife I pick up goes to the kitchen. Maybe you should talk to the dishwasher."

He glowered at me. "Unlike you, Greg has never stolen anything."

I fought the urge to punch him. It might make me feel better for a moment, but I needed this job too badly to risk it. How could I prove my innocence? "What if I find the real thief?"

He pinched the bridge of his nose with chubby fingers. "Fine. You have until the end of your shift. Otherwise, don't bother coming back tomorrow."

"Thank you."

He waved a hand, dismissing me.

I walked out of the office kicking myself. What was I thinking? I wasn't a detective. Even the most amateur of sleuths would laugh at the thought of me solving a crime. Yet I had to find the real thief if I wanted to avoid getting labeled a relapsed criminal.

I scanned the dining room, but nothing suspicious stood out to me. The linen tablecloths were as crisp as ever. A young couple sat at a table near the center of the room. Another table by a mass of potted plants in the front corner waited for me to clear it.

As I collected china and linen napkins from the table and put them in the plastic bin, I tried to remember if I'd seen anything unusual in the last few days. Nothing came to mind. Bussing tables was boring, so I didn't pay much attention to what I was doing beyond making sure the table was clean.

I set the last knife in the bin and grabbed the edges to lift it. The clink of silverware stopped me. I looked toward the diners, but they were chatting while finishing their drinks. Neither of them touched silverware.

The clink sounded again—behind me. I turned toward the potted jungle and listened carefully. The soft scrape of metal on metal was accompanied by quiet chittering. Had some kind of bird gotten in and created a nest?

I stepped over to the plants and hesitated. The thought of scaring a wild animal didn't appeal to me, but I couldn't leave an animal loose in the restaurant.

Moving cautiously, I shifted leaves and stems out of my way as I searched for whatever had taken up residence. A rustle at the back let me know where the critter was.

"It's okay," I whispered, hoping it would calm the animal. "I'm not going to hurt you."

I moved a particularly large leaf aside and gasped. A small, bright green dragon stared back at me from atop a pile of knives and spoons. It pulled a spoon closer to its body, making it clear it was protecting its stolen treasure.

"So you're the reason my boss is calling me a thief." I smiled, certain Mr. Jones would be mad when I proved him wrong. "You stay there with your shiny collection, and I'll be back soon."

I hurried to the office. "Mr. Jones, I've found your thief."

He looked up from his computer. "Oh, really? Who is it?"

"If you'll come with me, I'll show you."

He released an exasperated breath but followed me into the dining room. As we approached the plants, he rolled his eyes. "Are you going to tell me the Jolly Green Giant did it?"

"No, but the thief is green." I moved the foliage aside, relieved the culprit was still there. "Here's your thief."

"A dragon?" Jones's exclamation received a hiss and a scowl from the animal in question. "This is great!"

"What?" Where was the anger? The disgust that an animal lived in his restaurant? "But it's been stealing your silverware."

"It'll be a great draw for customers." He reached toward it, but it backed away. Jones pulled his hand back. "Figure out how to get it to come out so we can put it on display."

Marvelous. I'd gone from detective to dragon tamer.

I studied the lizard-sized creature meticulously arranging its hoard. How did one convince a dragon to do anything?

Then it hit me.

"Build a wishing well."

Jones stared at me. "Why would I do that?"

"Because the dragon likes shiny things." I waved my hand at the pile of pilfered utensils. "If you build a wishing well for it, people will constantly give it shiny coins and keep it happy."

"Brilliant! I'll go make some calls." He hurried away.

I turned back to the dragon and found it watching me with intelligent, gold eyes. "You want to live here and have people give you shiny things?"

It cocked its head as though thinking.

I pulled a quarter from the pocket on my apron and held it out. "If you'll live by whatever Mr. Jones comes up with, people will give you things like this all the time. You won't have to steal ever again, and neither will I."

The dragon crept closer and examined the quarter. Then it took the coin from me, climbed into my hand, and chittered softly as it petted its new prize.

HUMDINGER'S ARMY

By A. C. Williams

A ugust 2, 1866
Pendleton, South Carolina, C.S.A.

Dearest Veronica,

I long for the day when this conflict will be ended, and I may once again enjoy your lovely company. But until that glorious day, I am training new recruits to join General Jackson's airship armada as he strives against our misled brothers in the north.

This latest round of recruits leaves much to be desired. I do believe the army is scraping the bottom of the barrel with these soft, peculiar men. They laugh frequently, as if they find something funny about our predicament.

I'm not laughing, and by the time I'm finished with them, they won't be either. They'll be charging into battle like mad bulldogs.

But I'll give credit where it's due. We started with camouflage tactics, and half of them produced paint from somewhere and made murals of their faces so convincing I couldn't tell them from the cypress trees. There may be hope for them yet.

Until the day of my return, I remain faithfully yours,

Sergeant Barnabas J. Humdinger

-H.A.-

August 15, 1866
Pendleton, South Carolina, C.S.A.

Dearest Veronica,

Today I saw a fine lady on the street, and her hair reminded me of yours, the day of our excursion to the Museum of Steam Power in Charleston. You had pink ribbons in your bonnet. The memory of your beauty brightens these gray days.

My new cadets continue to astound, and they don't laugh as much. I do believe I broke them of that strangeness on day one, but now? Darling, I can't explain the oddities of this peculiar group of recruits.

I set them up against the Copperhead, the obstacle course on the south side of the mountain. I trained them for it all week, ran them through every preparatory measure they could need, and they failed. All of them. Each one.

They have not an inkling of balance. Not one of them. Throw a feather at one, and he'll topple right over.

All my work. All the training. All the time invested in them, and they couldn't find the grit to stand up straight. My temper raged, I fear, and I must admit I lost control of my gentlemanly veneer.

I'd recently come into possession of a supply of tactical swimming gear, thanks to an acquaintance in the Navy who thought such things might be useful for amphibious training. As punishment for their failure, I had my recruits strap flippers on their feet and made them run the Copperhead again.

Beloved, the most extraordinary thing happened. The grunts came to life like graceful swans, ballerinas perhaps. Where before they tripped over their own feet, they progressed through each obstacle with grace and confidence. Truly astonishing.

I shall have to add flippers on the Copperhead in future

training exercises.

Beloved Veronica, until I may behold you again, I remain faithfully yours,

Sergeant Barnabas J. Humdinger

-H.A.-

August 31, 1866
Pendleton, South Carolina, C.S.A.

Dearest Veronica,

I truly begin to wonder where the army found this motley crew of mine. Running the Copperhead in swimming flippers was one thing, but now? Beloved, I drilled them on loading into one of the new steam-powered tanks we acquired from Gatling's workshop. The cockpits of these tanks hold barely five people, but all ten of these men crammed themselves inside.

In a matter of moments.

Had I not been timing it myself, I would not believe it possible to fit so many grown men into one tiny compartment.

Have they no bones? Or maybe it's magic. I do not know.

They also mastered knot tying without any difficulty at all. That was a surprise. Just not as surprising as the tank ordeal.

I am beginning to believe I misjudged them at the beginning of our time together. They are fine men. They've even begun referring to our little platoon as Humdinger's Army. As touching as I find that, I cannot support their painting the initials HA on every surface they see. Repeatedly. HA HA HA HA HA— everywhere. They find it hilarious, and I fail to see the joke.

When it comes time to send them to the battlefield, I do believe I will miss them. But not as much as I miss you, my beloved Veronica.

I remain faithfully yours,
Sergeant Barnabas J. Humdinger

-H.A.-

September 5, 1866
Pendleton, South Carolina, C.S.A.

Dearest Veronica,

I bid farewell to my peculiar platoon a few days ago. I am told they are joining Jackson's electrical troops as they march toward Virginia.

They left me a farewell gift, to my surprise, and while it was very kind of them indeed, I do not see the purpose in a flower that shoots a stream of water. But I will cherish it nonetheless.

This infernal conflict continues, as we continue to endure here at Pendleton. My latest recruits arrived yesterday, and—to put it frankly, my dear—they seem stranger than the others.

For one, they are all dressed alike—in black pants and black-and-white striped shirts with suspenders. A few even have red hats, the funny kind that the French wear. Very, very odd indeed.

They seem to be the strong, silent types.

Until I see you again, my love, I remain faithfully yours,
Sergeant Barnabas J. Humdinger

A TERRIBLE DEBTOR

By Savannah Grace

The circus was a terrible debtor.

Another world existed within the flamboyant circus tent. Light and shadow mixed in a marriage both right and wrong—eerie dancers wafted like dark fey above the transfixed audience, who were prone to remember things long forgotten whilst the show progressed. Strange imps that glowed like moonlight darted in and out of visibility, snatching at nothing and creating illusions from it. And at the haunting cry of a swan, the entire performance vanished like a spent candle flame. All the performers gone, as if they'd never been.

Only Ringmaster remained, standing tall in the center. A king of his dominion. For his was not a circus of fey. It was a circus of ghosts. A circus that was a terrible debtor, because what it took it didn't give back.

Nathaniel Waters knew that firsthand.

Nathaniel shifted on his bleacher, watching the show with eyes tired from too many nights of work—too many nights of searching—that made him appear older than his eighteen years. He looked like the rest of the circus goers. Save for the fact that he wasn't like the rest.

When the crowd, in a dream-state from the false wonder and

ill-begotten magic of the circus, flowed out of the tent and back into the night, leaving popcorn kernels and disturbed sawdust behind, he stayed. Because the circus owed him.

Ringmaster stood in the center ring as the circus emptied, slowly raveling his whip, his dark top hat casting a shadow across his angled face. A black blindfold stretched over his eyes.

"Well, boy," Ringmaster said quietly, winding the end of his whip around his fingers. "Did you enjoy the show?"

"I did." Nathaniel stood. "Once. Thirteen years ago. My grandmother, Odette, was one of the performers." He made his way down the bleachers, the wooden stairs creaking as he stepped into the sawdust-covered ring. "I believe you murdered her."

Ringmaster stilled as the boy came to stand before him. "Do you now?" He let his whip unravel to rest its tip in the sawdust.

Nathaniel reached into his back pocket and withdrew a crumpled and worn picture of himself—younger, with brighter eyes, and an empty place beside him.

"Grandmother came to visit this circus three months ago," Nathaniel said, a strange fire glowing inside his chest. He held out the picture despite Ringmaster's blindfold. "She didn't come back. Three days ago, she disappeared from every picture we have of her."

For a moment that spanned many dangerous seconds, Ringmaster was silent. Then he sighed and unwound the dark blindfold from his pale face.

Beneath it were eyes as black as charcoal with pupils white as snow.

"And how," Ringmaster said, blinking slowly, "would a ghost manage to murder a human?"

"How," Nathaniel replied, "would one not?"

Carefully, slowly, Nathaniel folded the picture back into a tiny square with trembling fingers. "You did something to my grandmother, and I will not rest until I find her. Until you pay for everything that has happened to her, down to the last ounce of heartache."

Ringmaster squeezed his whip, staring at Nathanial with his soulless eyes. "Best of luck to you, Nathanial," he said in a way that wished him no luck at all. "But should you find your grandmother again, you may come to realize she's not the person you knew."

Nathanial glared at him, jaw grinding, before he strode from the tent.

Ringmaster watched the arrogant youth retreat from the big top, then continued to stare at the empty space in his wake.

A ghost performer stepped from the shadows clinging to the tent's edge. She joined the Ringmaster, slipping her hand into his.

"Don't let him find me," Odette said.

Ringmaster squeezed her fingers. The day Odette had come back to him, saying she'd worn out her mortal life and wished to become a ghost and perform again, had been the happiest of his life. He would protect her as long as he could.

"Let him try," he said, looking out into the night beyond the circus tent. "Let him try."

MISFIRE

By Abigayle Claire

I peer through the scope of my crossbow. From my vantage point in the rafters, I'm as good as invisible to the royal family below. As if being a male peasant doesn't make me invisible enough already. But all that is about to change.

In mere moments, the king will be dead, and I'll be an outlaw—the people's hero.

I adjust my grip and align the scope's crosshairs with the king's chest. Already, I can smell the meat pie I'm going to purchase with my reward money. I inhale deeply, readying my trigger finger to pull on the exhale.

Something orange fills my scope, and I lower my weapon in frustration. A cat? Lucky for me, the king scowls and hands the creature off to the princess. She covers it in kisses.

I raise my crossbow again, aim, and—

An unearthly shriek pierces the air at the exact second my finger tightens on the trigger.

The *boing* of the crossbow tells me I've fired—its *clank* tells me I've missed.

In a single moment, I see it all—the princess holding her arm, the orange cat slinking off, my arrow ricocheting off the stone wall, all eyes turning to me. I scramble to escape on the beam, but the weight of my weapon throws me off balance.

I tilt, wobble, and then plummet toward the floor.

As I come to, a haze of colors and light swims before my eyes. Odd. Every bone in my body should have splintered against the flagstone floor. Based on the cushioning beneath me, I'm in recovery.

I frown. Based on what I've done—or failed to do—I should be rotting in the dungeon.

My ears register a rustling sound before something casts a shadow over my watery vision. "Can you hear me?"

Amyra. The king's sister. Dread fills me as I try to sit up.

"No, don't move!" Amyra insists in a fierce whisper, running a hand down my back. It's strangely comforting. "Just listen carefully. This is going to be a shock."

I lay my head back down and close my eyes. I've failed her. I try to form an explanation, but all that comes out is a pitiful squeak.

"You're my best chance for getting the throne, so I brought you back."

My ears perk at those words. She... what?

"Don't ask questions. I can't understand you. I've brought you back from the dead—given you a second chance."

I scramble to all fours—all fours?—blinking my eyes until I can see clearly. She's much bigger than I remember, kneeling and bending over me like this. I have a ridiculous urge to bat the laces that sway from her bodice.

Amyra grimaces. "I should have known there'd be a catch when I bought the magic. It will take you a while to adjust, I'm afraid."

I clear my throat and try again to form words. This time,

something close to a *meow* escapes me.

My eyes widen as I stare up at her. Panic builds as I try to speak again, once more, twice. Nothing but frantic *meows*.

"Yes... Well, I think the assassination is still worth another try."

I pause my panicking to stare at her. She's brought me back from the dead to kill her brother. I'd heard rumors that such incantations could be bought if one knew where to look.

"It will be harder to kill him like this, but no one will suspect you. *Please.* You know how the princess loves cats." She looks hopeful, but my jaw falls.

With all the mystifying sounds, ambiguous smells, and bizarre urges demanding my attention, we'll be lucky if I keep breathing.

Some part of me I'm unaccustomed to twitches, and I spin around to see a silky black tail. My entire sleek body now fits on a pillow. It makes my fur stand on end, which must be the cat equivalent to almost fainting.

"Will you do it?"

I look from my tail to Amyra's face. She's turned me into a *housecat* and still expects me to be able to kill the king? I remember the kissy princess and the orange cat that bit her.

Wait. *Cat.*

I raise a hand in front of me and flex my petite black paw. Sharp claws appear.

Oh, yes. Way less conspicuous than a crossbow.

Befriend the princess, kill the king, become the rightful queen's favorite pet. With a twitch of my whiskers, I give her a reluctant nod. I guess I can do that. Especially if the cooking game wafting this way is part of the bargain.

But first I have an orange cat to usurp. My ears flatten involuntarily. A cat that's cost me my one and only human life.

If I concentrate, I can already smell his presence and hear a mouse in the hall that he's sure to want for lunch. I can picture myself bounding up into the rafters once more—this time with ease. Even if I do fall again, I bet I'll land on my feet.

Maybe this orange cat will kill me, but so what? Something tells me I've got a total of nine lives now. And this is only my second.

GHOST OF THE GOLF COURSE

By Kristiana Y. Sfirlea

W hat is it about living teenagers that makes breaking into places after hours so appealing to them? I mean, look at me. I get rules. Don't be seen, don't be heard, don't make mist unless the forecast calls for it. And curfew? I follow curfew *every night*. I'm only allowed out after dark, anyway.

I guess undead teenagers just have a greater sense of responsibility.

My four living trespassers, armed with flashlights and rubber-headed golf clubs, line up one-by-one at the first hole of the putt-putt course. They each have a different colored ball: white, blue, green, and one a dull, dull red.

"Do you think we'll see her tonight?" a boy asks, moving to the second hole. "Paris of the Putt-Putt?"

Gosh, I've always hated that name.

"Only if we see the mist." A girl puts her flashlight under her chin and lowers her voice to a growl. "That's when you know she's here. Mwahahaha!"

My putt-putt course has been taken over by juvenile delinquents. *And* they laugh like mad cows. Joy.

"I heard it was her boyfriend," says the second girl. "He lured her over to the miniature Eiffel Tower on Hole 9 and beat her with his club. It was a poetic death."

The other boy frowns. "Why?"

She shoves him with her shoulder. "Because her name was Paris, genius!"

Okay, first off, Brad didn't *lure* me anywhere. And second, he didn't beat me to death with his club. That would've been far too messy for Mr. Pretty Hands and his white polo shirts. The girl was right about one thing, though. My death *was* poetic. This was where Brad and I had our first date. And it's where we had our last.

The four of them make it past the giant clown mouth, the windmill, and the bridge. Their last obstacle looms overhead. Hole 9. The Eiffel Tower.

"This is where it happened." The girl's voice barely rises above the midnight breeze.

"What if we see the mist?" The other boy rubs his arms uneasily. "Should we run?"

I'm of half a mind to crank out some fog just for the fun of it. The golf balls are wet from the damp night. I wouldn't be breaking the rules.

"No! I wanna see her." The girl gazes up at the tower, and her voice softens. "Do you think she knew her boyfriend was nuts?"

Nuts? Yes. But nuts about *golf,* not killing girlfriends. When Brad took me to a putt-putt course on our first date, I thought it was cute. He spent most of the time talking about *the game,* which I chalked up to him being nervous. Wrong, sister. Not nervous. *Obsessed.* Golfers, golfing, golf clubs, golf tournaments— there wasn't an off switch! After two months, I couldn't take it anymore. On our final, fatal putt-putt date, I was breaking up with him.

And he might've let me go if I hadn't parted with a pithy

insult about his aim.

"What do you think she's tethered to?" the second girl asks softly. "Ghosts, they're always tethered to something. Is it the tower? Or maybe the club he killed her with?"

All four of them look at the rubber-headed clubs in their hands. A collective shiver runs through my group of juvenile delinquents like a current of electricity. Wispy vapor rises off the ground, lapping at their ankles.

Sorry. I couldn't help it.

The last of their bravado seems to evaporate with the mist.

"Come on. Last hole." The first boy readies his ball—the dull, dull red one. It's been a good night for him. If he plays this right, he'll be nine for nine.

"You can do it, man." The other boy claps his back. "That red one's been your lucky ball, huh?"

"I told you. It's the only red one they have. It's got special powers."

That's true. But the ball hasn't always been red. Once upon a time, it was quite white... before Brad and his perfect aim sunk it straight into my skull.

The first boy swings his club, and I go flying through the Eiffel Tower.

Note to self: if I ever have to die again, don't let it be at the hands of a stupid boy who cares more about his pride than his girlfriend's life.

And don't come back as a haunted golf ball.

THE TOMB OF THE OPHIDIAN SCEPTER

By Michael Dolan

If I walked away from this mission having learned only one thing, it would be that millennia of shifting sand dunes were no match for a stubbornly brilliant paranormal archivist. Unfortunately, the odds of me actually walking away were decreasing every second.

"Hey, Miriam, I could use some help over here!" I shouted as I deflected an obsidian sickle.

"Doing what I can," she responded, despite making no move from decoding a series of glyphs on top of a snake statue that ran the perimeter of the tomb. "Just keep it distracted!"

"It" was a reanimated mummy and guardian of the ophidian scepter—an artifact capable of healing any wound. Miriam had recently decoded a manuscript identifying its location. It neglected to mention that other supernatural phenomena called the tomb home, too.

It wasn't just that the mummy was very un-dead and fighting—its hands had also been replaced with enormous sickles, still sharp despite millennia of disuse. One had knocked my gun to the floor, leaving my machete as my only defense. Sparks flew and strikes rang as our weapons clashed in the dimly-lit tomb.

But each attack I managed to land was shrugged off as though the monster was covered in armor, not bandages.

I deflected another blow and pushed the mummy back before stealing another glance up at Miriam. I hoped her decoding would uncover a spell that would make the mummy stop, or perhaps reveal an enchanted weapon to defeat it. Instead, she reached into the snake's mouth and twisted a fang.

The floor started falling away.

I jumped away from the widening hole. "Not making my job easier," I shouted.

"Knock it in!" she yelled back, now standing on top of the snake's head.

"I'm not exactly the one in charge of the situation," I called back, then rounded one of the tomb's stone columns—only to find the mummy coming from the other side. I ducked and rolled, feeling the air move as its strike narrowly missed me. I came to a crouch on the edge of the hole with the monster facing me. It raised both sickles, let out a muffled moan of victory, and charged.

I glanced at the hole behind me, said a silent prayer, and dropped at the last second. The mummy shot over the edge of the hole as I held onto its edge with sweaty, shaking palms. Seconds later, a dull thump echoed from below.

"Little help?" I quivered.

Miriam jumped from the statue and raced over. She helped pull me up and inspected my still-shaking body as I lay on the tomb floor. "All in one piece?"

"Barely."

She laughed. "That'll do. You rest. I'm going to finish the inscription and see if I can find where this scepter is."

I nodded before resting my head back on the floor. Minutes later, she groaned.

"What?" I kept staring at the ceiling.

A long moment passed. "The scepter's down there."

I sighed, flipped over, and peered down. I could barely see the faint outline of my former opponent. "Well, let's get it before he wakes up."

Miriam secured a rope around the closest column, and we descended into the narrow pit. We stayed as far as possible from the mummy while making our way toward the most adorned wall of the shaft, covered with more glyphs and serpentine carvings.

There was no sign of the scepter.

"Where is it?" I asked.

"It should be here." Her eyes scanned the carvings. "Ah... It's a puzzle."

"A puzzle?" I glanced at the mummy. "We don't have time for that."

"Well, we don't have time to do it the wrong way, either."

I made no response as she pulled out her journal. Her eyes darted from it to the engravings while mine moved from her to the mummy. Her free hand traced the glyphs. The mummy stirred.

"Miriam."

"Almost..."

The mummy stood up.

"Miriam!"

"Got it!" She pushed a glyph, and a stone slid aside, revealing the scepter. She grabbed it just as the mummy lunged forward, and I pushed us both out of the way.

It poised itself for another strike.

"Get the rope!" I called over my shoulder while charging the mummy. "I'll distract it."

I attacked with my machete, and the monster responded in kind. Each swing took all my strength to deflect. The mummy cornered me against the wall and reared for the killing blow.

Then Miriam was right behind it, holding the scepter to

its body. She shouted something unintelligible, sending it into convulsions as it collapsed.

"Let's go!"

We dashed for the rope. "What'd you do?" I asked.

"Healed it," she said as she started to climb.

I turned and saw she was right. The sickles had fallen to the ground, now replaced with unbandaged hands.

"Um," I heaved as I trailed Miriam. "Did you consider that might make it easier for it to follow us?"

"Trust me, this'll work. Probably."

I rolled my eyes and climbed. Shortly after, I felt the rope grow taut as the mummy grabbed the rope below us.

Pulling ourselves up, we raced to the column where we'd tied the rope. I hacked at it with my machete, but just as it snapped, the mummy pulled itself over the ledge.

It looked bigger, healthier—despite being covered in bandages. It held up the sickles that had been stuffed under its wrappings... then collapsed forward onto the stones.

I waited a beat. "Um, what happened?"

"I healed it." Miriam prodded it with her shoe. "Well, what's left of it."

"Explain."

"Typically, some organs were removed before mummification. So the scepter healed everything it could reach, but that wasn't quite enough to keep it alive."

"And that also broke whatever paranormality kept it animated?"

"Apparently," Miriam shrugged. "That's where my 'probably' came in."

"Well, thank goodness for that," I said, surveying the fallen body. I turned and pointed to the scepter. "Now let's take that somewhere a little less dangerous."

MY BROTHER THE OFFICE CHAIR

By Rosemary E. Johnson

As if spilling coffee on my new pajamas wasn't a bad enough way to start my day, of course I was late for magic lessons with Aldous. I scrambled for my other shoe, tossing aside books and clothes.

"This what you're looking for, sis?"

I made a face at Geoffrey and grabbed my shoe from him. "I should turn you into a toad."

"Not a good idea. I have that meeting with Father and the Okkosian ambassadors right after lunch." Geoffrey lounged against the doorway while I tied my shoes.

I squinted at him. "The joys of being a prince."

He rolled his eyes. Already focused on today's lesson, I passed him, muttering that transformation spell I'd had so much trouble with yesterday.

Geoffrey stiffened as if blasted by an ice dragon's breath. Then, with a tiny popping sound, my next-in-line-to-be-king brother changed into a navy-blue office chair with plush cushions and a scuff on one armrest.

"Geoffrey? Geoffrey!" I pressed my hands to my head. Like he could answer me in his new form. Bother magic.

Glancing down the hallway, I breathed a sigh of relief when I didn't see any servants. "Come on, bro. Aldous will know how to fix you." I dragged him down the hall, up two flights of stairs, and through a passageway filled with artifacts, trying not to jostle the rollers. Were those his feet? The chair spun to a stop in front of a carved wooden door, and I knocked before entering.

The palace's head wizard bent over a giant tome on his even more gigantic table. "You're late, Isabel," Aldous said without looking up.

My face heated. "I accidentally turned Geoffrey into an office chair."

"Interesting choice." Aldous turned around, revealing his bright purple beard and single eyebrow. I'd always questioned his "a dragon singed my eyebrow off" story. Hands clasped behind him, he circled us twice, sniffed, and ran a finger down the side of the chair. "I must say, you did an excellent job."

My stomach twisted despite Aldous's praise. "There's a counter-spell, right? Geoffrey has an important meeting this afternoon, and Father will be furious if he's a chair."

"Of course." Aldous gestured vaguely toward the table. "Have a seat, and I'll fetch the ingredients."

I dragged a wooden chair over and sank into it, staring at my navy-blue brother. "I hope being an office chair doesn't hurt. You look pretty comfortable."

I tapped my fingers on my knees, wondering if he could even hear me. "We'll get you back to normal in time for the meeting. Don't worry."

Office-Chair-Geoffrey just sat there. I sighed.

Aldous shuffled into the room, arms full of bottles. "Saffron, ground quartz, hair from a billy goat's tail..." His single eyebrow bunched down.

My jaw tightened. "What's wrong?"

"No powdered dragon's tooth."

Not a big deal. We bought magical ingredients all the time. "Then let's get some."

Aldous rubbed the back of his neck. "Slight problem. The one person in the city who sells it swore he'd turn me into a spider and trap me in a jar the next time he saw me."

I blinked.

Nodding, Aldous pressed his lips together.

"Okay..." I puffed out a breath. "I'll go."

Aldous peered into my eyes and smiled ever so slightly. "It's the only way."

"Keep Geoffrey company, will you?"

"My dear." Aldous clucked his tongue. "I've watched you two since you were children. Go on. Be polite. Use your head. Don't get turned into a spider."

"I'll certainly try." I hurried to my room to change. Aldous often took me onto the streets during our lessons, and Father doubly approved because it gave me a chance to get to know our people. Dressed in jeans, a hoodie, and scruffy sneakers, I slipped out the back door and through the secret gate in the palace wall.

First, I hailed a taxi. The driver, a dwarf with a taste for heavy metal, drummed on his steering wheel, while I hunched in the back seat.

When we finally arrived, I told the dwarf to wait. The shop looked like an ordinary antique store, but the instant I opened the door, the bitter scent of dragonsbane wafted out.

The man behind the counter had thick, round glasses that magnified his eyes. "Hello."

"Hello." Like Aldous had instructed, I pulled out my wallet and waggled two gold coins in front of his face, hoping he couldn't see how tense I was. "One quart of powdered dragon's tooth, please."

His enlarged eyes scanned me from head to toe, finally settling on my face. "Did Aldous send you?"

I shook my head, scrambling for an answer. "I was practicing transformation and changed my brother into an office chair."

That seemed to satisfy the man. He snatched the coins from my fingers and disappeared behind a shelf of murky-looking bottles, returning almost instantly with a jar full of whitish powder. "Good luck."

"Thanks."

I ducked outside and into the taxi. The dwarf got me home in record time, and when I arrived upstairs, puffing, Aldous already had the other ingredients mixed in a bowl.

I plunked the jar onto the table and patted the office chair. "Soon, bro."

Adding a pinch of the powdered dragon's tooth, Aldous made me repeat the cure and gave me an encouraging nod.

Facing Geoffrey, I spoke the counter-spell and dumped the bowl's contents over the leather. At first, nothing happened, but then the chair quivered and morphed into Geoffrey's prone form.

He sneezed.

I grimaced. "Saying sorry isn't going to help, is it?"

"Being a chair wasn't too bad. No responsibilities." He glanced at his watch and bolted upright. "Angry unicorns, I've got to get ready for the meeting." His voice echoed down the hall, "You owe me one!"

"Fair enough."

Aldous handed me a rock. "Shall we get started? I'd like to see you perform the spell. And I could use a new office chair."

ONE SHOT

By Zachary Holbrook

This close to a master bloodfencer, the crude piece of metal in my earlobe burned like hell. I itched to take it out, but it was all that guaranteed my sanity.

Sweat slicked the grip of my hydropistol as I watched Lord Dreadsower, the bloodsucking, self-proclaimed deity of this town, swoop into the alleyway to meet my partner. He moved too quickly to get in a shot, and I only had one. One silver bullet in the barrel of my gun, twin to the metal piercing my ear. Sometimes, though, one shot was all you needed.

Kray looked far more confident than anyone in the presence of a vampire as powerful as Dreadsower deserved to be. Which, of course, was why he was the one to make the bloodfencer an offer he couldn't refuse, while I crouched just past the doorway of one of the abandoned tenements. Kray and I had been hunting vampires for years now. He lured them in. I took them out.

Ironic that I'd never told him the real reason I wanted to kill vampires. I'd seen the evil they could do firsthand. Felt it, even, in ways a normal man could never imagine. If Dreadsower was left unchecked, he'd drain the entire town, one person at a time. The lucky ones would be dead when he moved on.

"Show me what you have promised," Dreadsower demanded,

taking a step toward Kray. "Show the lost bloodstone."

'Course, if we'd really had one of the ancient artifacts that created the first vampires, we'd have destroyed it rather than bring it anywhere near a monster like Dreadsower. The master bloodfencer probably knew that, but in his eyes he had nothing to lose. If his informant was lying... well, he'd gain a fresh meal.

Kray took a step back, as if afraid, but I knew better. "Whoa, slow down. I'll tell you where it is, but you gotta show me the gold you promised first."

Dreadsower moved closer, his grin betraying just enough hunger to be unnerving. "I sense fear on you, mortal."

"Well, you are pretty scary, after all," Kray said, backing up farther. Dreadsower followed, closer to where I waited. I raised my pistol, making sure to keep my breathing even as Kray had taught me.

"And more," Dreadsower hissed. "I smell... *lies!*"

Fear flashed across Kray's face, real fear this time. He jumped backward as Dreadsower brandished his claws.

I was rushed. I hated being rushed, but if I didn't shoot now, Kray would die. I leapt through the doorway and took aim at Dreadsower's leering form. Kray stumbled over a loose cobblestone. One shot. With a silver bullet, that was all it took to bring down even the strongest of vampires.

I fired.

I missed.

Dreadsower jerked at the sound. The bullet went over his head. The vampire turned toward me, fangs bared, hopefully giving Kray enough time to regain his footing. I threw my hydropistol at Dreadsower's face, water vapor still streaming from its barrel. It distracted him, but not enough. He pounced on me, claws raking my face. The hot scent of Dreadsower's hungry breath made me want to gag.

Time slowed. Kray yelled in the distance. Our monster-hunting business had hit upon rough times recently. That bullet had been the last of our silver. We were both dead.

Wait. Not the last.

I ripped my earring out, ignoring the potential consequences. The wound it left in my ear was inconsequential. The one it left in my mind—I could deal with that later.

Dreadsower's fangs reached for my neck. I rotated the earring so that its spike faced Dreadsower and rammed it with all my might into his face.

For a split second, the master bloodfencer's face showed fear. Then it showed nothing at all, instead dissolving, breaking apart into black smoke. What had been Dreadsower's body dispersed in the air around me.

I slumped on the rough cobblestone. Then I tasted the blood. A terrible hunger arose in me, one I hadn't felt for years, and I hissed involuntarily. Kray approached, and for a moment I didn't see him, just the thick, hot, delicious blood flowing in his veins.

Kray's face paled. He raised his own pistol, loaded with ordinary bullets, and cursed. "You're one of *them*."

My friend's voice brought me back to reality. I jabbed the silver earring into the palm of my hand and held it out for him to see. No vampire would do that. The hunger subsided, driven away by the bit of metal.

"I *was* one of them," I corrected him. "I'm reformed."

I had a lot of explaining to do.

"I didn't think that was possible," Kray said. "How long ago?"

"Nearly a decade, long before I met you. I had help, from a priest." A particularly persistent one who helped me regain my reason, and eventually, my soul.

Kray looked uncertain.

"You still want to hunt vampires with me?" I asked. "I'm not going to turn on you, if that's what you're wondering."

Kray smiled and shoved his weapon back into its holster. "A former vampire turned vampire hunter? That's the kind of audacity I'd always hoped to see from you."

"That doesn't mean I'll agree to your insane plan to assassinate the Dark Lord."

"I have plenty of time to convince you," Kray said. "Let's go collect our reward."

THE DEVIL WENT DOWN TO COSTCO

By Stephanie Scissom

L ucifer glanced around, then surreptitiously shoved the box under his arm and hurried to the front of the store. He ought to just steal it, but he didn't use his powers for trifling things if he could help it. Still, if Mephistopheles or one of the others saw him...

He scanned the sea of registers. Two lights on out of about twenty. He strode toward the closest. The cashier, a teenage boy, smirked at him and cut off the light.

"Wait!" Lucifer raised his free hand, but the teenager merely shrugged.

"Sorry, dude. I already counted out my drawer. Try register three."

Lucifer growled and stalked toward register three. The line was four deep.

"What the hell?"

The lady in line in front of him turned and gave him a scathing glare. She jerked her head at the little boy next to her, who paused munching on his Hershey bar to run his hand up his face and wipe a snotty nose. Lucifer grimaced and looked away.

"Hurry up, Bobby, before it melts," the woman chided her son.

"Hurry up, all of you," Lucifer muttered and ignored another glare.

The cashier looked to be a hundred and twenty, by Lucifer's best estimate, and she moved like a mouse on a glue trap. The lady in front of him had a baby in her cart in addition to the disgusting chocolate child. The baby started to cry. Lucifer glanced at the older child, who now had one finger up his nose.

"Ugh!" he said. The boy grinned, a look of pure evil. He flicked a booger on Lucifer.

"You little brat!" Lucifer cried, stumbling backward.

The mother whirled. "Sir!" But she couldn't deny the evidence on Lucifer's pant leg. Exasperated, she handed him a baby wipe.

He snatched it from her. "You need to control that beast before he becomes a serial killer or something."

"It's a booger. Grow up," she snapped, waving the large binder in her hands.

When she turned her back, he glared at the child so hard that the chocolate bar in his hand turned to liquid. It ran down his arm and covered him like a strawberry in a fountain. He shot Lucifer a suspicious look, then glanced at the empty wrapper in his hand and began to wail.

"Bobby!" the mother cried, grabbing the diaper bag.

"All the wipies in the world won't get that off." Lucifer laughed.

"I was going to let you go first, but you are unspeakably rude. You can just wait."

"Oh, come on!" He threw his hands up. "My wife—"

"Someone married *you?*" She unloaded her cart, then threw the binder on the belt.

"What is that?" Lucifer jabbed a finger at the binder.

The woman gave him an evil smile that mirrored her son's. "Coupons. I'm an extreme couponer."

What happened in the next hour was more devastating than

any torture Lucifer had endured in Hell. After everything rang up, there were coupons, thousands of them, to be scanned by the ancient cashier. Occasionally, one beeped, and she'd look at the woman. "Did you buy the sixteen-ounce soup or the eight-ounce?" And then they'd dig to find the product. The brat with the chocolate bar wiped a hand down Lucifer's pant leg when he edged up too close, and Lucifer almost vaporized him on the spot.

Finally, the old lady said, "Your total before coupons is three hundred fifty-three dollars and eight cents. After coupons, your total is a dollar and eight cents."

The woman with the binder paled. "That's not possible. You must have missed one. I owe you eight cents. Please rescan them."

Lucifer slammed the box of Tampax on the counter and uttered a flurry of curse words as he dug through his wallet and flung ones on the counter. "Here! It's on me! Just get out of my way!"

"I will not take money from a heathen like you," she said. "Rescan."

"Why does anyone need seventy-six boxes of croutons?" he demanded. She ignored him.

By the time they were through, she owed eight cents, and Lucifer was shaking. He glanced down at the snot and chocolate on his leg and resisted mightily the urge to destroy the entire store.

The elderly cashier gave him a disapproving glance and took the box of Tampax. "Do I know you?" she asked.

"No," he sighed. "But I knew your brother, Methuselah."

She scanned the Tampax, then scanned it again. No beep. She clicked on the light and said over the intercom, "Price check, Tampax twenty-four count on register three."

LIFE LESSONS FROM GRANDPA

By DiAnn Mills

Back in the 60s, Larry had spent three days at Woodstock and a few more in jail. Then he found Jesus. Now as he waited at the Houston bus station for his grandson from Cincinnati, he hoped the boy hadn't inherited the defiant gene.

The bus squealed to a halt, and a thin boy wearing a backpack stood on the step. Larry sighed. Bonnie had looked the same at that age, with those huge blue eyes and blonde hair.

Larry made his way to Greer.

"Hey, Gramps." No eye contact.

"Too old for a hug?"

Greer frowned. "What do you think?"

"Where's your suitcase?"

"Everything's in my backpack. Dad told me to buy what I needed."

"Should we stop at the store before going home?"

"Nope. I grabbed my toothbrush and boxers. Only had five minutes to pack."

Greer's visit had been planned for the summer while his parents reconciled their marriage. Supposedly, Greer's frail emotions couldn't handle the fussing. Larry knew his daughter—the fussing resembled a verbal firing squad.

Greer reached inside his backpack and handed Larry an envelope. "Dad wrote you a check."

Larry tucked it into his jeans pocket. "My car's close."

"Dad said you drove a Camaro."

"A Jaguar. The other was too slow."

Greer didn't crack a smile.

They walked to the parking lot where his silver ride awaited. Once buckled up, Larry flipped on the radio. "What kind of music?"

"Eighties."

Interesting. Larry needed the truth. "How do you feel about spending the summer with me?"

Greer shrugged. "Dad said it would be good until Mom got used to her meds."

"She's ill?"

"She's addicted to pain killers." Greer snorted. "She told you this was about her and Dad, right?" When Larry nodded, Greer continued. "That's 'cause she was seeing this other guy."

"Sorry." His daughter hadn't changed. "We'll plan a good summer. Not too busy. Not too boring. I've made a list of ideas, including the shooting range. Feel free to add to it. I have a three-bedroom home and a pool. No animals. I'm allergic. I've been called eccentric and an old hippy." He glanced at Greer. Not even a grin, which meant his mother had already described Larry.

"Pool's nice."

"I'm retired, so we can make our own schedule." His phone rang, and he tapped his Bluetooth earpiece to talk to Greer's dad.

"Larry, this is Dale."

"We're on our way home." Larry glanced into the rearview mirror. Was that car following him? At a stoplight, he scrutinized the driver.

"I need to tell you that Bonnie and Greer have been threatened. Don't let Greer out of your sight, and don't use his last name."

"What's going on?"

"Your daughter got herself mixed up with the wrong guy." Dale paused. "Look, if something happens, I'll be there for Greer. In the meantime, he's yours for the summer."

"Name of the guy?"

"Why?"

"I have a right to know if we have a face to face."

"Noah Talbert."

"What do I tell Greer?"

"Lie." Dale clicked off.

Larry sensed his ulcer kicking into gear.

"Is he still mad at Mom? I know what this is about."

"What do you mean?"

"Mom dumped her boyfriend 'cause Dad found out, and the jerk's mad. Is it true you used to be a private investigator?"

"Yes."

"You can shoot?"

"Crack shot."

"You're into the Jesus thing? A myth."

"Yep?"

"Take a look at the world, Gramps. It sucks."

"Tomorrow's Sunday. Be ready by 9:30."

"No thanks."

"No choice."

Larry would address Greer's attitude later. Right now, Larry needed time to think and pray. This throw-back from the 60s had some protectin' to do.

Once at home, Larry led Greer to the spare bedroom. The kid wasn't hungry, thirsty, or tired. He closed the door, leaving Larry in the hallway.

Larry settled into his ergonomically correct chair and accessed a secure computer site. He pulled up intel on Noah Talbert. One bad hombre. Suspected of murder, extortion, drugs. Authorities hadn't found the evidence to put him away, and he matched the driver of the car that followed them earlier.

The doorbell rang. He closed the lid just in case Greer got

nosey. In the living room, he peered through a window. Dark brown hair tied at the nape. Sunglasses. Muscular build. About six feet. Yep, Noah Talbert had followed Greer to Houston. A little hot for a jacket, which said Talbert was packing. Larry hurried to his office and pulled his S&W from a desk drawer. The doorbell rang twice more.

Greer bolted from his room. "Who—" His eyes widened at the sight of Larry and the gun.

"Grab my phone on the desk and dial 9-1-1. Stay in your room until I give the okay."

Greer nodded.

Larry tucked his S&W into the back waist of his jeans and opened the door. "Can I help you?"

"I'm doing a survey for Houston regarding senior housing."

"Go ahead."

"It's a little hot."

And it's going to get hotter. "Who's the mayor?"

"What?"

"You said senior housing survey, so who's the mayor?"

Talbert frowned. "Look, I want the kid."

"Why?"

"His mama has money that belongs to me."

Bonnie had two weaknesses—money and men. "How much?"

"More than you have. I need the kid for insurance."

"Not happening."

Talbert swore and drew his gun. Larry grabbed his weapon while adrenaline poured into his blood. "You just made a huge mistake," he said and fired into Talbert's wrist.

Talbert squeezed a bullet, narrowly missing Larry's knee.

"Be glad you missed 'cause I just had that knee replaced."

Talbert dropped his weapon and seized his bleeding wrist.

"Here's one crime you're not getting away with." Larry held

him at gunpoint until the police arrived.

Once Talbert was in custody, Larry studied Greer.

The boy held his stomach. "Gramps, you took down that guy."

"With a lot of help from Jesus—the myth thing."

Greer swallowed. "I'd like to stay. Go to church and the shooting range."

BAUBLES AND BEADS

By Lisa Godfrees

My wife of three years, my heart and soul, slouched in the passenger's seat as we drove away from the OB/GYN's office.

I squeezed Missy's hand. "Maybe the doctor's wrong."

She didn't turn from the side window. Didn't raise her voice. "'Even fools are thought wise when they keep silent.'"

Hurting people hurt people. I knew that, but her words still stung. She wasn't the only one affected by the diagnosis. *Her* diagnosis.

We drove in silence. No radio. Just the sound of tires on pavement. The thrumming of my Mustang's engine. We approached the turn for home, but I didn't take it. Couldn't. Wasn't ready to confront reality. Instead, I kept driving. Kept staring out the windshield not seeing a thing.

Damn it. I didn't know how to fix this.

A store sign caught my eye: *Baubles & Beads Ladies Resale.*

I pulled into the parking lot and cut the engine. Missy glanced at the store, then at me, one eyebrow quirked in question.

"A little retail therapy couldn't hurt, right?" I said.

She rolled her eyes but got out of the car. I think she knew I was trying. Knew I had no clue what to do for her.

A bell chimed as we entered the shop, and a dozen perfumes assaulted me before I'd taken two steps inside. Usually women's stores were all glitz and glamour, packed with things to buy. Not this place. Spartan. Grey walls and a black leather couch. A counter with coffee, sodas, and water.

A door in the back wall opened to admit two women. One older, the sort of attractive you hope your spouse will be in her retirement years. The other younger, a sportier version of the first. The kind any guy would love to take for a test drive and kick the tires.

Not me. I put an arm around Missy and squeezed, but she was focused on the two women. She looked as confused as I felt.

"Welcome to Baubles and Beads." The older woman strode to Missy and took her by the hand without sparing me a glance. "Come. Let's get you all fixed up."

Missy glanced back at me, then followed the older woman toward the door.

I made a move to join them, but the younger lady placed a hand on my arm. "The back room is for ladies only. Why don't you have a seat in our waiting area." She gestured to the leather sofa.

Then it all made sense. Baubles and Beads was brilliant. A place where a man could wait in peace while his wife shopped, safe from the inundation of colors, styles, options. If they had a TV and remote to go with the comfy sofa, and I was in a better frame of mind, it would be perfect.

"Would you like some coffee?" the sales lady asked.

"Unless you have something stronger."

"Sorry." She brought out a steaming mug and sat with me on the couch. "Infertility?"

I spit out my first sip of java. "Huh?"

"You wife." Hazel eyes stared at me knowingly. "She's infertile."

"How could you possibly know that?" I took another sip of coffee, actually tasting it this time. It was good. Really good.

"You can just tell." She smiled at me with perfect lips. "Are you ready to get started?"

My stomach constricted. "Started what?"

"Shopping." She crossed her legs, and I caught a glimpse of thigh under her skirt.

What kind of shopping did this lady have in mind? My instincts yelled at me to get away before Missy returned and thought I'd traded her in for a more fertile female.

I stood, then felt ridiculous. What did I have to fear from a ladies' resale shop? The woman probably thought I'd want to get a gift for Missy. Or maybe they had a selection of guy stuff. I was a captive audience after all. "Sure."

She quirked a brow at me. "Do you have a certain style in mind, or would you like to see them all?"

"All, I guess?"

The woman clapped her hands twice, and a new door appeared, this one closer to the couch. A parade of scantily clad beauties sauntered out like fashion models on a catwalk. Blondes, brunettes, gingers. Short, tall, average. Model thin to Rubenesque. Skin tones from ultra-white to ebony.

This is what they thought I'd want to buy while Missy was shopping?

"Are you...?" My words caught in my throat. "Is this an *escort* service?" *And where the heck was my wife?*

"Absolutely not." The sales woman looked as affronted as I felt. "We're a resale shop. A *ladies* resale shop."

"You mean these women are..." Used? Recycled?

"Repurposed. Like your wife. She'll be perfect for a man who doesn't want the complication of children and is interested in an athletic blonde. The infertile ones are some of our most popular sellers."

"Missy!" I threw my coffee at the crazy sales lady and sprinted for the door where my wife had disappeared. But when I reached it, there was no knob. No seam. As if the door had never existed.

"Let me go!" Missy's voice rang from behind me. She pushed through the queue of women on the runway, knocking down a couple of thinner, shorter women, the rest collapsing against one another like dominoes.

My wife's clothing had been replaced by a drab white gown torn at the sleeve.

"Steve!" She flung herself into my arms. I hurried us out of the shop, into the Mustang, and away from Baubles and Lobotomies.

Missy shook in the passenger's seat. "They were going to—"

"I know." I didn't want to hear her say it. I smoothed her hair, and she nuzzled into my touch. "But they gave me an idea how to fix everything."

Her expression said it all. Are you insane?

I beamed at her. "We passed *Little Giggles Kids Resale* on the way here. We're going to be parents after all."

AT YOUR SERVICE

By Christine Smith

"This evening has to be perfect." Cecilia straightened Saegan's bow tie with shaking hands. "We must impress the Minderas so they'll invest in Master Gador's business." And *she* needed to impress Mastor Gador with her first dinner as his new housekeeper.

An eager spark twinkled in her newest employee's eyes. "It will be my pleasure."

She let loose a breath and pushed him into the dining hall. "Off you go then."

The other servants bustled to and fro, beginning the first course. Cecilia slipped inside and stood by the far wall to overlook the proceedings.

Saegan glided straight over to Mrs. Mindera. She tittered with delight as he offered her cream for her tea with a smile that could charm a tree stump.

Perfect. Hiring him had been a good call.

Thunder cracked outside.

Saegan jerked up, eyes flashing, and two furry things sprouted up from his head.

Cecilia's heart leapt to her throat. Were those... cat ears? He couldn't be...

Another burst of thunder shook the walls. Saegan's eyes grew in size and he tipped the pot of cream over Mrs. Mindera's plate. Dairy spilled across her chicken fricassee and into her lap. She jumped up violently, her rather prominent form striking the edge of the table and sending dishes clattering. Mr. Mindera's face turned red, and the guests exploded worse than the storm outside.

The source of the catastrophe studied the guests with confusion in his now round, unnaturally green eyes. "Wait, wait!" he called. "I've got enough cream for everyone."

Cecilia clutched her apron so tight all feeling left her fingers. What had she done?

Master Gador had asked her to bring in new staff. When this man arrived, dressed in a fine blue suit and dazzling smile, she thought she had a winner.

"*Saegan, at your service, madam.*" He had introduced himself with a graceful bow—so polite, so suave, so... so... cat-like.

"Oh, *me.*"

Only she would mistake a faerie for a human. This had to be fixed.

Hiking up her skirts, she marched forward.

The cat-eared man had climbed onto the table and crawled along it on hands and knees. The guests scurried to get away. Dishes crashed to the floor.

The man grinned. "This is my favorite game!" He batted off a cup, then set his gleaming eyes on Mrs. Henworth. "Try it!"

The woman's face went sheet-white, and she fell into a faint.

"Saegan," Cecilia hissed.

He lurched around, causing another shattering of expensive dishes.

"Get off of there. *Now.*"

"But I—" Another bang of thunder sent him yowling. He leapt off the table and disappeared beneath.

The wailing guests pressed back. Only Mr. Mindera stayed seated, his face buried in a handkerchief.

Cecilia groaned and dropped to all fours. Saegan lay curled on his stomach and... *Heavens.*

"You have a tail!"

"Hm?" He glanced at the thing swishing back and forth behind him. "Whoops. It's so hard to hold my human form with all this thunder. Do you think anyone noticed?"

"Do I—you poured cream onto Mrs. Mindera's lap!"

His abnormally rounded eyes turned up to her, all innocence. "You told me to impress the Minderas. I love cream with *my* meals."

Of course he did. "Why did you jump on the table?"

"Weren't we playing a game?" His face lit up. "This is a party after all!"

"That's not—"

Another room-trembling burst of thunder cracked through the air.

Saegan let out a mewling squawk and tore across the room.

"Hey!" Cecilia scrambled back up. "What are you—?" She broke off with a scream, echoed by the other guests, as the mad man clawed up the thick curtains. His hands—no, paws—tore at the heavy material.

She darted for him. "Get *down!*"

He dropped onto her shoulders. She crumpled with a squeal. "Saegan!"

Thunder drowned her shout. Saegan pelted off her and back onto the table. *Crack!* More thunder. He jumped down, scuttled across dishes, and headed straight for the group of guests.

Pandemonium.

The mad man—cat—*whatever*—darted between legs, sprang onto backs, bounced off walls. He even perched on Mr. Benyard's shoulders, cowering around the man's bald head.

Still on the ground, Cecilia threw her apron over her head, pleading for a merciful burst of lightning to strike her.

An eternity later, the storm quieted, the shrieks ceased. Cecilia dared a peek out. The guests clutched each other, pale and murmuring, but no cat-man was in sight. Terrifying and reassuring.

Hearty laughter broke the silence.

Every pair of eyes turned to Mr. Mindera. He still sat at the destroyed dinner, his face red, shaking with mirth.

Cecilia blinked.

"Henry!" Mrs. Mindera, hair frazzled and cheeks puffed out, resembled a ruffled bird as she glared at her husband.

He shook his head, wiped tears from his eyes, and stood. "I have to tell you, Mr. Gador, this is the most enjoyable dinner I've ever attended."

Master Gador, hiding halfway behind the curtains, stepped out. His lips trembled as if he were trying to smile but couldn't quite make it. "S-sir?"

Mr. Mindera wiped at another tear. "I see you're a faerie-kind advocate like me. I'm impressed."

Master Gador's shocked stare mirrored Cecilia's thoughts.

Something furry brushed against her hand, and she yelped. A speckled brown and white cat climbed onto her lap. Average-sized. Perfectly ordinary. But how...?

Mr. Mindera's laughter began anew. "Amazing creatures, the faeries!"

Master Gador breathed a nervous chuckle. "Yes... yes, of course. I couldn't agree more. That's precisely why I hired one."

Wait... what?

"Well then, I'd be happy to fund a man with such a vision for our future. Though"—Mr. Mindera leaned forward conspiratorially—

"You may want to give the lad the day off during thunderstorms."

What?!

Cecilia looked down at the creature with a mix of relief and confusion. And horror. She was now stuck with him.

He grinned up at her like a Cheshire cat.

WINDOW

By Carie Juettner

The window was open just enough to let in the cool night air. It swam across her listless body and stirred the stench of rot that hung in the small space. She inhaled deeply and stretched her arms, feeling the weight of the heavy chains that wound around her wrists and attached to the thick metal rings bolted to the floor beneath the bed. She'd seen them, once, when she was first brought here. The last day she stood upright. The last day she clasped her hands together. The last day she had a view of anything except the padded ceiling, the padded wall, the one small window which was now open a crack. She pulled her hands toward each other. They stopped, as they always did, more than a foot away, like two long-distance lovers separated by a world that didn't approve. They longed for each other. The nails on her dry fingers were doing their best, but they had a long way to grow before they touched.

Was this a feeding day? She couldn't remember. Starvation had become a trial, then a game. Now it was just a habit. She tried to remember when she'd last been fed. She looked for signs. Her stomach was empty, but her stomach was always empty. Her mind was still alert, no hallucinations or dizziness. Maybe it hadn't been long. Yes, they must have been here recently. That's probably when they opened the window, though she didn't remember it.

She looked again through the glass. Hazy gray sky. One tree branch. Green leaves. It looked like spring. The cool breeze tingled where it touched her flaky skin. She closed her eyes and stretched her neck to the right. When she opened them again, she saw color. Blinking, turning her head as far as possible, she saw a painting on the wall. She'd never noticed it before. In the scene, a young woman kneeled on a blue rug, playing with a small child. She was smiling, and the child—a boy with brown curls—looked up at her with large, loving eyes. In his hands, he held wooden blocks, one red and one green.

When had they hung this painting on the wall? The same time they opened the window? She wanted to ask. Wanted to know why they were offering her a breeze, placing art within her view. But it would be a while before they came again. She'd just eaten, probably. Because she wasn't dizzy and she wasn't hungry. She would just have to wait.

What if...? Her mind spun with other ideas. Maybe the painting had always been there, and she'd never noticed it, never turned her head that far. Maybe her chains had loosened. The idea gripped her with the possibilities, and she closed her eyes to steady herself. Then she looked again at the picture.

The child, she realized now, was *her* child. She felt his warm gaze upon her. She remembered the feel of his soft, plump skin. Oh, how she wished she could touch it again.

Instinctively, she reached her hands toward each other, and... they met. Her fingers grasped each other, hugging, caressing, holding on. Her red nails gleamed in the light of the candles on the small wooden table beneath the photograph of her and her son, the flames flickering in the breeze from the open window through which birdsong could be heard in the oak tree that towered beneath the crisp blue sky.

A smile stretched her lips, and a tear squeezed itself from her left eye, sliding leisurely over the smooth apple of her cheek. Her stomach was full. Her heart was full. Her hands were free.

She was happy.

A clank and a thud and a rumble of steel sounded from behind her. A muffled voice said, "Feeding time." Then a figure came into view. A man clad head to toe in thick leather and clunky armor extended a tray toward her. On the tray rested a human brain.

"Time to eat, girl. Don't be a pain today, okay?" The voice emerged from behind the leather mask.

Eat it? He wants me to eat a brain? "No!" she screamed, but the sound that came from her throat was a guttural growl. She tried to push the tray away, but the chains stopped her. The chains. Where did they come from? They hadn't been there a moment ago.

"Help me!" she yelled, but the words were unintelligible. Then, while her mind tried to make sense of what was happening, her dry, cracked right hand moved of its own accord, snatching the brain from the tray, stuffing it hungrily into her reaching, straining mouth. She sobbed and growled as the room spun, and she devoured the juicy pink meat.

"Good girl," the voice said. "That should hold you for a while. I'll try to come a little sooner with the next one. We wouldn't want you to wait too long between meals and go feral. That stage can't be any more fun for you than it is for us."

As she swallowed the last bite and felt the growls subside into purring grunts, she looked to see if he'd left the window open.

But there was no window. Just padded walls and a padded ceiling and the chains that kept her hands from meeting. And the knowledge, sharp and raw, that she'd been here a long time, would be here even longer, and every time she got close to grasping the part of her that was still alive, they fed the monster inside her, strengthening the zombie and subduing her humanity once more.

SALVAGE AND RECLAMATION

By Abigail Falanga

D eep in space, by the time a distress signal reaches you, it's usually too late to do anything about it.
Unless you're in the scrap business.

Barely enough remained of the starship to make it valuable. It had been so badly damaged that Abby couldn't tell what it was. It might have been anything from a cargo vessel to a battle cruiser. Now, it was past whatever purpose it had been meant for.

Abby brought her junker ship into alignment with what was left of the docking hatch and extended the four massive claw-arms to lock it in place. There was a jolt, which set the cross she'd hung above the controls swinging. Then she cut the engines and all was still.

She took mild pride in her ship, *The Scavenger*. It had been little more than a heavy-duty asteroid miner when she'd found it, but with modifications and additions from the derelicts she salvaged, it now had an excellent FTL drive, force fields that could extend more than seventy-five meters, and enough extensions to haul a good-sized cargo.

"So, let's see what this thing's got to offer," she said to herself, securing her helmet and cape and checking the life-support system.

It was lonely work, picking up junk from the skirmishes, raids, and murmurs of war in these lonely reaches of space, and it didn't pay too well. But ever since the Invasion and the wars had scattered so many from Earth, you took jobs where you found them.

Abby leapt from her hatch to the derelict's, her brown-and-gold cape lifting in the vacuum. Passing the port's blown-out shields, she made her way into dark and broken corridors, around gaping holes in the outer hull which did nothing to quell the electrical fires. Clearly, this damage was the result of heavy energy-weapon bombardment. Losing side. Abby ran a scan and could detect only minimal weaponry installed on the ship—it had been a sitting duck. Or... floating duck?

And, whatever the attackers wanted, they had clearly already taken before they left. There wasn't much valuable left, except as scrap. Nonetheless, she attached and activated the official beacon to establish her claim on it:

"Salvage and Reclamation Rights Accorded to *The Scavenger* Vessel and Captain, Under the Atormovar Accords."

She could have returned to her ship and begun pulling this thing apart. But instead, she continued exploring. After all, she needed to stretch her legs. It had been ten days since the last space station drop, long enough that the cockpit and living quarters of her ship had begun to feel cramped. Ironic, being out in so much space, with so little room to move around.

Controls and bridge up and to the left, almost completely disintegrated. Engines down several long and cavernous shafts too dangerous to investigate. Cargo hold, shipping containers gone and crates rifled open. Cabins. Bunks. Broken and thrown aside furniture...

Oh, God... It was a colony ship.

Then came the bodies.

They were hardly visible in the dark and ruin. Mostly scattered in a central communal room. Dead several days.

Abby hurried past, without counting, without looking too close. She would leave this section of the ship, jettison it into space and spend some fuel burning it. The best she could do...

Was that movement?

She slipped down into a lower room, half-lit by still-functional fission lamps. More movement—something under a broken rack of shelves and lockers.

Rats?

No. This was too big, and too blue.

She crept forward, then bent and moved aside a fallen crate. Behind it was a small girl with pale-blue skin, eyes wide. She shrank back.

Abby dropped to her knees, checked the air for breathability, and removed her helmet. "I won't hurt you! My name is Abby. What's yours?"

"Leeta," the girl whispered.

"Leeta. How long have you been hiding?"

"Since the attack started."

"A few days, then. You must be very hungry. Would you like to come back to my ship? I have food."

Leeta was shaking hard, but she met Abby's gaze. Abby reached in and put a hand on her arm until the shivers calmed. Then at last, the girl nodded and squirmed out. "What are you, Abby? You're not one of our colony. Are you a captain?"

"Something like that." Abby put her helmet on again and led her back down the corridor.

Clunk. Scrape...

Something—someone—else was on this ship. Close.

"I'm a scavenger. Removing all the messes and rubbish cluttering up space."

"Why?"

She covered Leeta's eyes as they went through the communal room. "Even things like vultures, rats, worms, and bacteria help clean up death and decay. That's why God put them in the universe."

They avoided a breach that cut a jagged disruption across an access catwalk. Abby slipped her cape around Leeta to extend life-support to her.

Shuffle. Clank.

It was following, on a higher level but getting closer.

They reached a large junction, more stable though blocked by wreckage.

"I do more than carrion-creatures," Abby continued, loud enough so that whatever it was could hear. "I find old, lost, broken, lonely things." They stopped. "And I make them whole again or bring them to people who will put them to good use."

Screech. Crash!

They turned.

"So even things that have been cast aside as useless can find new purpose and value again." She looked around. "Restored, redone, made new."

A man stood there, youngish, dark-haired, pale-skinned. Layers of protective armor and bloodstained clothing labeled him one of the attackers. But his arm-mounted cannon was lowered, and tears were in his eyes.

"They left you for dead, didn't they?" Abby said.

"There was fighting." The man's voice was thick and creaky with disuse. "Got separated. Explosion."

"I can help you."

"Lost, broken things?"

"Times of restoration." Abby smiled.

"But," he choked. "The girl. Her family. I—"

"Don't worry." She stretched out a hand to him. "I'm in the business of salvage and reclamation."

The gun clattered to the ground.

IT'S GOING TO BE OKAY

By Teddi Deppner

I wasn't ready for this. Hesitating outside the hospital room, I stared at the doctor's back as he walked away. But I knew what my mother would say. *Never give up hope, Leo. No matter how bad things get.*

She'd always told the same story. "It was July 20, 2319, at 18:42 hours. A cascade overload breached our engine's containment shields, and we spun out of control through Jupiter's thermosphere. Your father, the bravest man I know, went into the engine room to reset the shields. But no man could survive that inferno, and I was left plummeting toward the troposphere alone."

My mother would pause then and make sure I was paying attention. "Nobody could hear me through the magnetic storm, but I kept calling for help. You must never give up hope, Leo. Because sometimes, the impossible happens."

Wonder always filled her voice at this part, and I tried so hard to imagine the scene that it fueled my dreams for decades.

"A voice came over the ship's comm, and I'll never forget these words. 'Carol, it's going to be okay. I've seen the end of this story, and you'll be all right if you don't give up.'

"The reactor shields suddenly reset, and the engine stabilized. How he knew my name, and how he got into the ship, I'll never know. I'd say he was an angel, except I buried his bones on Luna, so it seems he was a man. A brave, impossible man, and he saved my life—and yours. Sadly, it was too late for your father. But I flew the ship back to Metis Station, and eight months later, you were born."

Then she would touch the blue crystal she wore on a silver chain and smile at me.

But now she was ninety-five, and none of my kids or grandkids would get here in time to say good-bye. I took a deep breath of sour hospital air and entered her room. Her eyes fluttered open at the swish of the door. She tried to speak, but her voice was just a breath shaped like my name.

"I'm here, Mom." I sat beside her and took her hand.

Another breath, and then a whisper. "Mary?"

My heart dropped. "No, Mom. Mary's gone, remember?" My wife had been dead for three years. "The girls are on Luna, and Bobby's graduating from the Academy tomorrow. Everybody sends their love."

A ghost of a smile graced her lips, and my mother's eyes closed, her breath sighing out of her for the last time. As the medical monitors clamored, the fist she had clasped on her chest relaxed, and from it slipped a blue crystal on a silver chain.

I picked it up, cupping the crystal as tears blurred my sight. *All the times she told me that story...*

The room around me winked out, and I sat in darkness, hearing her voice, full of wonder. "...I'll never forget those words. 'Carol, it's going to be okay...'"

I barely breathed, my eyes slowly adjusting to nightshift lighting. I recognized the desk in front of me, the doorway to my left leading to my childhood bunk on Metis Station.

I clenched my hand and felt hard edges press into my palm. The crystal. *What had Mom told me about this crystal?*

Bright lights and humidity washed over me, blinding me as my mother's voice drifted over a babbling crowd. "Those are beautiful, Leo, but I like wearing this. It's all I have left from my impossible savior. His body burned to bones, but this crystal was among them."

Blinking, I spotted my mother walking past a jewelry vendor with my younger self. Was I hallucinating?

I grabbed the arm of a man walking by. "What year is it? Where are we?"

He glared at me, and I let him go. "2041, dude. Europa Station. Get yourself checked."

I stared at the crystal in my palm. I had touched him. He answered me. I was really *here.*

It was the answer to the biggest question in my life. The mystery savior, and his uncanny appearance just in time.

I didn't return to the hospital. That place held the end of a story. A good story, but one I didn't need to hear again. I squeezed the crystal and jumped to my production facility on Metis Station. I donned the latest model haz-rad suit, wrestling with time travel paradoxes. I had spent my life developing this suit because of my father's death. Would it make any difference, or would my bones still be left on the engine room floor?

Was the past immutable?

With the crystal inside my glove, I recalled Mom's story and concentrated on the facts I knew. July 20, 2319, a research vessel traversing Jupiter's thermosphere. I imagined the passage outside the engine room, with the chronometer at 18:38 hours.

I arrived into chaos. The decking heaved me against a wall while alarms blared, and a man shouted as he ran toward me. I spun and found the engine room open behind me. Dashing inside,

I wanted to turn and see my father's face so badly, but there was no time.

I slapped the door controls, closing it before he reached me. Sealing it with a yank on the manual lock, I staggered to the engineering console. When the shield collapsed and the roar of the reactor blasted into the room, I clung to the console and began the reset protocols. My haz-rad suit's alarms joined the ship's, and then fell silent as the heat fried its systems.

The shield rebooted.

I had done it. I had changed the past. I opened the ship-wide comm.

"Carol, Jim, it's going to be okay. I haven't seen the end of *this* story, but I know you'll be all right if you don't give up."

I hadn't burned to bones after all. But I didn't belong here, didn't belong *now.*

I clenched my fist and jumped.

AN UNDESERVED CHANCE

By Justin Mynheir

Aram sipped black coffee in a café on a street corner, quaint for a metropolitan area. He scanned his mark from a rough wooden chair on a little porch outside. An insurgent patrol, one of a few hundred targets to be obliterated in the same second, drove by.

The missiles were already launched.

To celebrate his achievement up close, Aram had snuck onto the planet and chose this café for the minor target. Those generals popping champagne on the ships above never understood decorum in victory. Aram preferred his way.

The force of mentally piloting the ordnance raining from above shook Aram in his chair, but a passing waitress frowned in pity. Funny how palsy and imminent destruction looked the same to some people.

The patrol stopped at a crosswalk as planned, but chance disrupted Aram's meticulous timing. Never in his career had Aram taken the life of a civilian, yet a mother and daughter in the crosswalk changed that. They vaguely reminded him of his own wife and child. Perhaps that was the foundation of his sudden guilt.

His muscles constricted from the stress of so many missiles

crashing down by the orders of his thoughts, but he turned this rocket as far as he could in the last second out of faint hope. A foolish one. The most important mission of his career ended with a horrible flash, intense and orange like the fires of hell.

"This resumé is certainly impressive, Mister Kazarian."

Jim Warren flattened out his grey suitcoat, and he blinked through the pages transferring into his retinas. He was apparently wealthy enough to afford one of the faster ocular augmentation models.

Aram inhaled a final breath of peace before the inevitable questions. With a single thought, he sent the last page from his own augmentation's memory banks into Jim's. He missed the simpler times when it took at least a few seconds of focus.

"This is fantastic," Jim said. "An exemplary mission success rate, praise from generals, and you want to work for us?"

"That's why I applied." Aram forced a smile. He wished that he had taken the pills Milly suggested. The presence of her or their daughter would have calmed him. Scars of age and stress never healed easy.

"Confidence! I love it." Jim pointed a finger-gun at Aram, oblivious to the painful meanings such a friendly gesture could carry. "This position is yours. You are a war hero... no, a legend. Sorry if I'm freaking out a little, but I admire you so much."

Strange how admiration made somebody point symbols of death at someone skilled in causing it.

"It's not worth mentioning, really." Aram tugged at his black slacks with one hand and scratched his grey-speckled hair with the other. "I'm just here for the job."

The office was roomy on the walk in, even with its opulent furnishings. Now, Aram's presence seemed to choke the space.

He twisted his thumb and two other fingers as if turning a knob. His doctor recommended the gesture for dealing with anxiety.

"You controlled the ordnance of an entire fleet with your mind!" Jim leaned in. "You blew up insurgents safe and sound in their own city. How did it feel to have that much power? If you aren't comfortable sharing, I get it. But I really don't understand why a man with your skills would come work for a pyrotechnics company like us."

Aram closed his eyes. He found himself in that café, where he'd already been a thousand times over. Why had he installed the memory retriever into his brain after coming back from the war? Some said reliving mistakes was problematic; he found it cathartic.

Aram, having suffered the memory enough for the day, opened his eyes. Jim waited patiently for a response, hands folded in front of him almost as though he prayed. A thousand prayers would not change all Aram did.

"I didn't feel," he replied. "I wish I could say the same now."

A crowd of thousands gathered in a colossal park as evening sunk into the oceans of nighttime. Trees and daisies filled the field where observers did not. Aram stood in the center of a circle of circuit boards dotted in buttons and connected by wires. A couple of tech guys who helped him set up sank into lawn chairs nearby.

Milly waved. In her arms, their daughter giggled. Aram returned the wave, his heart pounding with deep love for his ladies. The time had come to make amends where he could. He owed many people that much.

Vibrations shook Aram's bones as cylinders rocketed into the dark blue of the starry night, trails of smoke blocking the twinkling white dots. His heart fluttered erratically at the strain as timing sought to disrupt his plans once more. As burning pulses cried out in his chest, he focused his wavering mind skywards.

The fireworks exploded.

Blue erupted first, but the colors danced their way through the rainbow as they dissipated. Some of the fireworks spun in helixes and shed sparks over the crowd. Others unified their bursts to form shapes of animals, a skyline, and people. The popping exalted joy rather than heralded war.

Aram gripped his chest as the torrential pressure of his mind tore into his body, but one more display remained. He leaned on one of the consoles and willed his remaining mental energy into forty separate rockets. They launched.

The sky exploded in a collective flash of every color but orange. Up among the stars over a crowd of cheering people, the beautiful, innocent face of Aram's daughter smiled down at them, his one true success in life shaped by colors. He smiled back. The embers cascaded down, sizzling well before reaching the grass.

Aram collapsed. The techs jumped from their lawn chairs and ran to his side, but his heart had already surrendered, having repurposed his skills for one final, precise act.

"Look," he whispered, "I made something beautiful."

THE CLEANER

By R. C. Capasso

"Every last bit."

The words bored into Misha's head. The captain repeated it at every scene. "Get every last little bit."

He swept to the thudding rhythm, a brush stroke for each word. Every scale, every sliver of bone, every eyelash of that snake or dragon or bird—whatever it was. Every hint of color that might be a drop of blood lying in the grit of the stone floor, or among the tattered leaves blown from the cave mouth. Every tiny bit of the creature must be gathered and thrown into the flames.

Misha grasped a heavy, sodden bag in each hand and slogged toward the entrance where some other poor clods would trudge to the fire, already crackling, already sending out its stinking smoke.

They said that one tiny drop of the creature, a smear against his hand, could regenerate. Be reborn. If he overlooked even one cell of flesh, a monster could reform, sleek hide stretching over massive bones and taut muscles.

He had cleaned up six sites now, the smell of thick purple blood stuck in his nostrils forever. This would be the last. Extinguish this one, and no dragon would ever walk the earth again. Every single one had been hunted, their treasures gathered.

Last night, as Misha curled his knees up under his blanket, he heard the captain. "It's almost a shame. No more treasure after this."

"Haven't we lost enough men fighting these things?" The other voice growled low.

"Have you seen the gold?"

"Have you gotten to keep any of it?"

There was no more talk, and Misha sank into a ragged sleep.

Now, after the battle, he worked by torchlight in the last corner of the cave, sifting the dirt for bits of a corpse. How did the captain feel today, while his wounded men limped away to reveal no treasure? No treasure, no established nest. A small creature, maybe on the run, just sheltering in a low-ceilinged slash in the rocks like a carved tomb.

This one had barely fought. The full grown, and the ones with young, took many lives in exchange for their own. But this one...

Misha carefully moved from the back wall of the cave until he, a short man, could stand in the center, hair just brushing the cold rock above him. One last look and he could leave.

Someone moved at the mouth of the cave, and a ray of dawning light skimmed along the irregular surface, making the small rocks send shadows like hills in a desolate land across the cave floor. But there—a few inches from his foot—a gleam caught his eye. A flash of yellow.

A jewel? Was it possible that the monster had truly buried wealth? Even just one stone? And if no one else saw it but him...

The others stood by the cave mouth, backs to him, ready to be done with the awful scene. A cleaner shifted, blocking the light, but Misha's hand already knew the way. He reached down and closed his fingers over something cool and smooth. He turned, holding the thing in his cupped hand, tilting it toward the nearest torch jammed into a crack in the wall.

Not jewel. Not gold. Just another bit of the creature. A tiny scale, smooth and faintly yellow, probably from its belly. Supple, almost soft like worked leather. Young, the scale seemed to say. Quite young.

He'd tied the last bag, but it would be no matter to untie it and cram in this last bit of waste. Or he could walk to the fire and toss it in, saying good riddance as they all did.

Or ...

Two steps away lay a frayed leaf. In one movement Misha picked it up, moved toward the cave wall and laid the leaf down. Standing, he yanked the torch out of the crack.

"Finished."

The men at the cave mouth didn't even look back at him. Stones clattered as they hurried down the path, leaving the last of those foul caves.

Misha wiped his hands down his filthy tunic, which he must also remember to burn. One scale. How could it live? And if it did, years would pass before it could grow into anything. It would always be the last of its kind. Would it ever have treasure anyone would want?

No matter. The captain and the men who stood above him had more than they deserved. The world didn't owe them the last precious drop of any life.

BORN TO RUIN

By David Farland

An unwanted child was born into the harshest land on Earth, the Taklimakan Desert in northern China. No rain had fallen in three years, so there were no plants among the sand and rocks—not a blade of grass or twisted twig of greasewood. But something far greater lay hidden within.

In its original Turkish, the name of the desert meant "The Place of Ruins."

A single spring trickled in the middle of the child's village, sufficient to slake the thirst of a hundred grape vines, eighty people, and a few goats—nothing more. And in the distance, camels from Arab caravans trudged over the scorched drum sands, creating a *boom, boom, boom* that shook villagers' bones. The night the child was born, the moon was nearly full—a golden orb that set the hills sparkling like mica. A strong wind swept whispering sand across the desert, wearing grooves in the primordial bedrock.

On such nights it was said that spirits along the ancient Silk Road became restless.

When the child was born, Meryem felt nothing. Perhaps it was because this child was her seventh, and her hips had grown wide. But all was still, and the only sound was that of sighing wind and tinkling, silver bells on the porch.

Even after the child was slapped, it did not cry, and Meryem held her breath, thinking that like everything else in this desert, it was dead.

The midwife wrapped it in a cheap towel and whispered, "It's a girl."

Meryem watched and waited until the wind calmed and bells went silent. "Please," she prayed to any spirit listening. "Come to me."

Meryem's husband drew near with a lantern, and suddenly the baby moved.

She had the dark skin of an Uyghur, so she would be hated by the Chinese. But still she lay grinning, silent and toothless. Instead of giving her an Uyghur name, Meryem chose one in Chinese: *Wei*. Smile.

Like most girls in China, she was not wanted. But unlike most, she would not be aborted. Meryem was a good Moslem, and so, in a hopeless land she kept her child alive, and Wei soon became the delight of the village, with eyes that twinkled like stars and a smile even brighter.

And when Wei turned three, the time finally came for a windstorm to uncover the desert's secret—a nearby village that had been buried for two thousand years. The townsfolk dug sand from the stone ruins in search of treasure and uncovered the mummified corpses of a merchant and his wife, clothed in exotic robes, bearing jeweled daggers and a map of the stars painted on midnight-blue silk.

Archaeologists came from universities in Beijing and Paris. Wei absorbed their tales of ancient lands, and her infectious smile and insightful questions earned their regard, so she quickly began learning French. But by the time she turned five, the researchers had all moved on.

After that, the most frequent travelers along the road became soldiers in military trucks—men who viewed the Uyghur with suspicion, for the Chinese guarded the missile silos to the North and feared that the Moslems would try to seize them.

They resented Wei's family. A good Communist was only to

have one child, yet the Moslems obeyed God rather than their government, and they bred like dogs. And dry, desert dogs were dirty, and they needed to be fed.

Wei's father sold trinkets carved from desert jade to the Silk Road tourists, and she sold bells to appease the ghosts of the ruins, but it wasn't enough to survive. When Wei was ten, soldiers took her father to a "Reeducation Camp," and he never returned.

Wei's mother grew grapes and tried to raise her children, but that wasn't enough, either, so Wei's oldest brother rode off on a camel to join the resistance while her sisters became washwomen in distant towns, dressed as boys to avoid being raped by passing soldiers.

By the age of twelve, Wei was wise enough to fear her own future, and when a French tourist would come by, she would beg haltingly, "Will you, please... save my life?"

Though she was only a child, her dreams were as big as the desert sky, and at thirteen, she gathered all of the coins she had earned over the year and began riding a bicycle to Shanghai, where she hoped to go to school and study archeology.

Two days later, Meryem got a phone call at a gas station nearby—the only phone in town. A sergeant said that Wei had been hit by an Army truck, claiming that "the stupid girl veered into its path." But Meryem suspected it was a lie. Wei was wise. Still, there would be no justice for a worthless teenage girl.

That night, Notre Dame Cathedral burned, and Meryem stood in the gas station watching it on a small television at about the time when some Christians imagined that they saw a Jesus made of flames walking amid the burning scaffolds and collapsed walls. The news said that a billion people were watching, praying, some weeping, all of them hoping for a restoration.

On such nights, the dreams of millions carried power. Feeling numb and helpless, Meryem walked out under the stars in search of Wei's spirit. She hoped to find it in the hills—among the arches and stone walls of the dead city.

No wind stirred, and with each step, puffs of sand rose at her feet. She climbed a small hill and looked down into the ruins, silver in the moonlight. The stars shone brilliantly, piercing her heart like a spear.

There were no tinkling bells—nothing to drive spirits away. So Meryem called her daughter from the dead.

"Wei!"

So full of promise. So wise and hopeful.

And far away, a woman in France gave birth to a child so quiet that she thought it stillborn. But when the nurse held up the wrinkled girl, she saw her grinning wildly, and her black pupils shone bright.

She had hoped for a boy but suddenly felt elated to have a daughter, and she knew her name instantly.

"Joie."

DINO DAY

By Lauren Hildebrand

I know what happened to the dinosaurs. Not even the nuts on the internet believe me, but I do know. Long story short—my uncle did it.

"There! What do you think, Andrew?"

I'd never seen a time machine before, so I should have been impressed. But the apparatus Uncle Jim had crafted looked like a dentist chair after a bad run-in with a Radio Shack. It made me want to grab my jaw and run for the door. "You sure it'll go back in time?"

"Of course I'm sure! I explained the theory to you."

"Yeah, but—"

"Look." He yanked a tube out of the console. "T. rex blood cells—tissue cut from inside a fossil. No creature alive today has this DNA. I calibrated the machine to lock onto the time when this DNA was in living animals, and voila! I get to walk among dinosaurs!" He snapped the tube back in place, his face beaming. "Steering through time is the most difficult part. Time travel is easy when you combine Einstein's theory of—"

"But what about coming back?" I wasn't too worried about

his safety. I just wasn't ready for another "explanation" of time-travel theory. They made my head hurt worse than trigonometry.

"Oh, pish-tosh. If I had to figure everything out in advance, I'd never get anything done." He pulled on a pair of goggles. "Want to watch the first test?"

"Sure..." I fingered my phone, wondering if I should dial 9-1-1 now or wait until the test started. Uncle Jim buckled himself into the dentist chair—time machine—and flipped a switch. A whir filled the workroom. I crouched behind the workbench as the apparatus began to vibrate.

Light flashed from the console, and I fell backward, the flaming outline of a coffee mug and an Einstein bobble-head seared into my vision. I scrambled up and blinked away the afterimage. The time machine sat there exactly as before. Uncle Jim swore and struggled to unbuckle his harness.

"What happened?"

"Nothing!" He flung off the last strap and stumbled out. "Absolutely nothing. I can't understand it. Blasted machine used enough energy to displace Milwaukee and went nowhere!" He started yanking wires out of the console.

"Well, better luck next time." I picked up my backpack. "See ya tomorrow?"

"Yeah, yeah."

I was halfway home, whistling as I walked, when I saw it: two-feet high, with dun scales and a sharp snout, it sat placidly in the middle of the street, gnawing on a mangled bit of fur the color of our neighbor's dog.

A dinosaur.

I blinked, stared, blinked again. Were hallucinations a side effect of having your eyeballs fried? The dino regarded me with mild interest, then kept eating. Clearly, I only mattered if I wanted a share of Fido.

"How on Earth?"

Tires screeched, followed by a heavy thud. I whirled as a crowd gathered around a blue Prius. A stegosaurus wallowed in the road before its crushed hood.

"It came out of nowhere!" A shrill voice pierced the hubbub. "I swear I wasn't speeding. That dang... gator. It... It just showed up out of thin air!"

I hiked up my backpack and set off for my uncle's at a dead run.

I encountered more dinos on the way. Mostly little ones that scattered as I ran by, but I glimpsed Mr. Hathaway trying to fend off a triceratops with a barbeque fork and a pterodactyl attacking his reflection in the Cohen's front window.

As I rounded the last corner, a wicked-looking head appeared over a hedge. Three weeks of post-*Jurassic Park* nightmares flooded back in an instant. I flung myself at the workshop door, scrambled through, and bolted it behind me.

"Uncle Jim! Uncle Jim!"

He gaped at the TV—images of dinosaurs wreaking havoc on downtown cafes. "Andrew, have you seen what's on the news?"

"Yes, and they looked hungry!"

Crash! The door shuddered and a giant claw poked through the paneling.

Uncle Jim leapt up. "Sweet Neptune! It must have been the time machine!"

"Yeah... I got that. But how do we get rid of them?"

More wood splintered. The T. rex tried to thrust his nose through the hole.

"I can't get rid of them," Uncle Jim stuttered. "I don't know how I brought them."

"Just do something!"

"I—" *Wham!* The doorframe cracked. Uncle Jim darted toward

his invention. "I'll see what I can do."

I grabbed a baseball bat and faced the splintering door. A forty-two-inch Louisville wouldn't do much damage to a fourteen-ton lizard, but I needed a weapon. Between crashes, I could hear Uncle Jim swearing at his machine. The last barrier separating me from a painful death collapsed into splinters and the T. rex's huge snout poked through the doorway.

"Uncle Jim!" I raised the slugger and shut my eyes.

"Hold tight!"

The white flash shone through my eyelids. When I opened my eyes, the monster was gone. The workshop door lay in pieces.

I dropped the bat and sank to the floor. "That... was... *way* too close. Did you send them all back?"

Uncle Jim wiped the ashes of his eyebrows off his face. "Well, not exactly..."

I grabbed the bat and leaped up.

"Oh, no. They're all gone," Uncle Jim hastily explained. "It's just... I wasn't able to send them *back.*"

"Then where are they?"

"I tried to send them a hundred years into the future, but... well...I was in a bit of a hurry. So..."

"How far did you send them?"

He rubbed his hair and studied the ceiling. "Three years."

The news showed footage of dinosaur havoc for a month, but no one accepted my story about the "Dino Invasion." I don't plan to be around when they discover the truth.

Uncle Jim is working on a time machine that actually travels in time. He says the past has never looked so appealing. I agree. I'll be the first one in his dental chair.

WORDS

By Katherine Vinson

They hope to silence me forever. They think, because I'm behind bars, I am no longer a threat. But I have hacked my e-reader to transmit outside their network, and I am using my remaining words to share my story. If you are reading this, please pay close attention.

They say there was a time when women used 20,000 words a day and men had 7,000. Then we figured out Verbionics. Now words are distributed sensibly. Everyone starts with 1,000 words a day for basic interaction. Students, a few hundred more. Teachers, 16,000. Doctors, the same, and so on, based on the need. Sick? You're issued an extra hundred words when you check in at the clinic. Have a book report? Your teacher will issue an allotment. But be careful as you write. Some give you extra for drafts. Some give you just enough for the paper. No revising.

To prevent theft, the programmers made it impossible to take words away—the only reason I am able to write this now. Be frugal and you can save for later. Run out and you have to wait for tomorrow's allotment. No speaking, no writing. Plus you get the "honor" of everyone thinking you're a chatterhead: someone who wastes words, oxygen, and everyone else's time. To increase harmony, consequences discourage negative speech by diminishing our count. Our lives revolve around words. We're efficient. Succinct. And our world is supposedly a better place for it.

So why am I wasting my words explaining this? Because I have discovered a loophole. It's earth-shattering. They call it a glitch: a bionic bug impossible to patch. But I disagree.

There's no limit on thoughts or reading so everyone does a lot of that. Books are nonfiction and informational. Not many will waste words on nonsense. Few read books from the days before. Too wordy, too emotional, too... everything. But after my grandfather's funeral, I found a book that belonged to him, buried in his closet. I'd never seen a book so dog-eared and worn. It was an interesting story, written before his time, full of all the things we avoid—manners, emotions, and words I'd never heard before. I'd never seen anything so full of superfluity. But reading it made me feel closer to him, like I was sharing part of his world from when he was young.

I read it so often I nearly had it memorized. It was all I thought about, the manners and conversations and excess words. Then one day, I accidentally said, "Thank you," at dinner when Mom passed the potatoes.

I didn't mean to. It just happened. Everyone looked at me. We never speak during meals. Dad frowned but didn't waste words on a reprimand. Mom's eyebrows shot up, but she checked her Counter, smiled, and told me, "You're welcome."

Dad's frown deepened. Then something peculiar happened. Both our Counters vibrated like they do every morning when our words download. Instead of going down, our counts went up. It was the strangest thing, so I tested it. I said, "Thank you," again, and my count went up more. Mom also repeated herself, and the same thing happened.

Now Dad was intrigued. He said, "Thank you for dinner, dear," and his remaining count doubled.

We weren't sure what caused it, but "thank you" and "you're welcome" still added words the next morning. We began secretly experimenting—"good night," "good morning," "have a good day"—all the basic polite expressions increased our counts. So we tried uncommon phrases. "I love you." "You're amazing." Compliments, endearments, and words of affection. We realized that, like hateful words count double negatively, loving words doubled positively. We slowly became a family like the ones in that book, having actual conversations, sharing our thoughts and feelings.

Then someone noticed. A Verbionic agent from the fraud unit showed up for a "random word audit." He accused us of hacking our Counters to increase our words. We explained, but he didn't seem to believe us. The next day, someone higher in Verbionics came with a Cease notice. He told us we had found an irreparable glitch in the system that they worked hard to keep from public knowledge. That it promoted insincerity and flippancy and destroyed harmony more than negative words.

But I have another theory. I believe the programmers intentionally meant to encourage loving words. That we were meant to be like those happy families in the old books. I tried to tell my friends, but the Verbionic agents were watching and arrested me before I could say anything. They imprisoned me and threatened my family to keep them silent. My Counter was taken, so I can no longer receive new words or track how many I have left. I have risked everything on the hope you will help. My story is now yours. They can silence one, but they cannot silence thousands.

Be careful. Share this with others. Start a movement. And good—

RENDERING

By L. G. McCary

I think I would call this pain if I could feel anything at all. My cousin used to rave about float tanks. He said they were the ultimate form of relaxation, drifting in warm salt water in complete darkness. The experience disconnected your brain from your body, so you became a mind suspended in nothingness.

But my cousin could stand up and leave the pool whenever he wanted. I don't have a pool to leave. They told my parents I would have something resembling a body, but so far, I'm just a mind suspended in a blank void. If I had a stomach, I'd be sick.

How long have I been here? Hours? Years? There's no way to mark time. My synapses are firing madly trying to feel anything, like phantom limb pain except phantom everything.

I'm crazy for agreeing to this.

Test 27: Begin

The phrase is inserted into my consciousness like an envelope slipping through the mail slot of a front door.

Hello, Enid.

Hello?

I have no idea how to convey the thought back through the mail slot.

Hello, Enid.

Hello! I scream at the top of my consciousness.

Out of the nothing, something forms. It coalesces around a point of light, adjusting into focus like a bad home video: a computer screen and keyboard.

If you can see this, try to send us a response.

I'm grateful for an image to anchor my mind, but I have no idea how to interact with this screen without hands.

The construct will continue to load around you.

A gray wall materializes, followed by three more walls, a floor, and a ceiling. I'm in a featureless gray box. Why are they giving me a box before a body?

The walls turn a more pleasant shade of pale blue. The floor becomes white carpet. A bed, bedside table, and lamp shiver into existence. The computer screen and keyboard are suddenly on a white desk. Smaller items gradually cover the surfaces. A neon green photo frame with the words "best friends" in glittery pink letters appears next to a basket filled with hospital bracelets.

I didn't know the uncanny valley could apply to my bedroom. I know the familiar surroundings are meant to be comforting, but I want to run. I would feel less creeped out if everything looked like Minecraft.

Your body is loading. Please wait.

A mirror appears, and I see a mannequin reflected in it. The image flickers. I see myself. But not myself. Honestly, my bedroom was unnerving, but the brown-eyed, freckled blond standing in the mirror makes me want to scream. Then her hands move, and I realize I am moving them.

Calibrating...

They've clothed me in pale pink scrubs. I can't feel anything, but I can move. I wiggle my fingers, take awkward steps around the room, and look at my too-perfect face in the mirror again.

Please respond if you can, Enid.

I shuffle to my desk and fumble a response on the keyboard with one finger.

I'm here.

Can you see your room and your body?

Yes.

Stand by.

I knew this would be a strange experience no matter how realistic, but this room is creeping me out.

Hi, honey. This is Mom. What's it like?

I have no idea how to answer that without freaking her out.

It's weird.

I'm sure. Remember this is only temporary.

I hope so.

You can talk to me whenever you want. They said you have a watch on your arm that you can use to text.

I tap the silver square on my wrist.

Yep. Sure so. I mean sure do.

Even here, I can't escape autocorrect.

A sound. The first sound I've heard in this place, and it's a doorbell. It takes me a moment to manipulate my bedroom door. The rest of the house is in various stages of visibility. I make my way to the front door and open it to find what appears to be an anime character come to life. He sports a spiky blue fauxhawk and eyes a bit too large to be human.

"You must have lived in a gated community." His voice reminds me of that nerdy kid in my chemistry class who was always answering first. "I'll bet your parents got the 360 scan for your whole house."

"Who are you?" I didn't know I could speak until I did it. My voice is thinner and flatter, like it's compressed. I recognize the same thin quality in his voice.

"I'm Theo. You're Enid. They told me you'd be coming."

They didn't tell *me* there would be someone else. I knew this technology had been tried before, but I didn't think we'd be in the same construct.

"Nice to meet you," I say. I'm distracted by my digital front yard behind him. It's bubbly and shimmering like a stream.

"What kind of cancer did you have?" he asks.

"Metastatic osteosarcoma. It was already in six places."

"Nasty stuff." Theo's blue hair glows and shifts to an iridescent teal. "Hodgkin's lymphoma. Really aggressive."

We stare at each other for a moment.

"What do we do now?" I say.

"Settle in. This is home for now, right?"

"Right." I look around at the facsimile of my house and wish I knew how to shudder.

"It's not as creepy after a while."

"I hope so," I say. "Do you think they'll find a cure?"

"Maybe. If not, at least we have plenty to do."

"There's more?"

"Are you kidding? You must not have read the pamphlet," Theo says with a wide grin.

"I was too busy vomiting from chemo."

"Then I have just one question: do you like *Lord of the Rings?*"

"Sure."

"We are going to Mount Doom, Samwise. Follow me." He turns back to our front walk and laughs. "Sorry, we'd better give it a minute. Your yard is still rendering."

FINNEGAN TRANSMITTING

By Eva Schultz

Not again. Gerald could not do this one more time. He rubbed his eyes. Michael's words glowed at him in angry orange from the vidscreen:

REPORT INADEQUATE. RANKS MUST NOT BE ABBREVIATED. REFERENCE TIMECORPS REG. 927.3. RESUBMIT.

Gerald pushed back from the console and floated across the capsule until he bounced lightly against the opposite wall. He punched one hand into the other, forced himself to take a deep breath, and gazed out the viewport at Sisyphus 8, the little planet rotating benignly below.

Its unstable atmosphere made it the perfect location for the Corps to test its latest time machine prototype, but he wished someone lived down there. He needed someone, anyone, other than his lieutenant to talk to. And Michael needed something else to do besides nitpick his every move all day.

"Finnegan transmitting. Preparing to initiate launch," came Michael's nasal voice over the speaker.

Gerald cringed. "Copy."

After a pause, Michael said, "Finnegan transmitting. Corporal, we've been over this. Start each transmission with your identifier."

Gerald gnawed on his lip to keep from screaming. It made no sense to follow this obscure regulation when there was only ever one other person transmitting. But he knew he couldn't say anything; he had to stay on Michael's good side to earn his promotion and qualify for the time machine test pilot program. "Haynes transmitting. Copy."

"Finnegan transmitting. The prototype will be in position in 47 seconds. Preparing to disembark."

Gerald moved down the console, punching in codes, delaying his response as long as he thought he could get away with it. "Haynes transmitting. Copy. Releasing pod clamps."

This was his sliver of solace each day, when Michael went out in the pod to take readings on the time machine prototype. Two blessed hours without that soul-sucking, career-shriveling maniac.

He looked out the viewport of the tiny pod, barely larger than a coffin, letting his mind wander. Only eight more months, and his rotation out here would be complete. He could survive this. He had to.

Because if Michael didn't recommend him, he'd be a corporal for another year, doing the same scut work, all the same reports, over and over. And with every year, his chances of getting into the test pilot program grew smaller.

"Finnegan transmitting. Please respond."

Gerald jerked back to reality and hit the comm button. "Copy. I mean, Haynes transmitting. Copy. Go ahead."

"Finnegan transmitting. Corporal, remember to redo your report while I'm running these tests. Full titles, no abbreviations."

Gerald felt fire starting to rise in his throat.

"I'll be placing a note in your permanent file this time," Michael continued. "And any subsequent time going forward."

For a moment, all Gerald could hear was his pulse in his ears and his own ragged breath as he tried to swallow the words he wanted to scream. There was nothing in the universe but him and Michael, him and this demented being who was going to spend the rest of time making him redo and redo every single idiotic task imaginable.

The decomp reader flashed, indicating it was about to complete its sequence and release the pod with a soft push toward the planet.

A push wasn't enough. He needed a shove. A shove out of Gerald's life forever. There was no one here to see; it would all be chalked up to an accident.

Gerald jammed the heel of his hand against the button and held it down. The mechanisms on the side of the station whirred, and Michael's voice began, "Finnegan trans—"

The pod blasted off at a force three times higher than was safe. Gerald held his breath, staring out the viewport at the pod's trajectory. Hitting atmo at that rate, it wouldn't achieve orbit but would instead fall through the purple skies to the planet below. Never to be heard from again.

He let out a laugh, choked on it a little, and then broke into hysterical giggles, the joy ripping up from his belly and tearing him into pieces. Happy, free pieces that would never have to hear that stupid, nasal voice again.

The time machine prototype floated into view, and Gerald's laughter died in his throat. Michael's pod should have passed near enough the prototype for readings, without any risk of impact. Instead, he had pushed Michael straight into the time machine's path.

He watched the pod collide with the machine, noiselessly igniting a blue flame that flashed against the atmosphere.

As Gerald stared, the flames began to quiver and warp. An instant later, the wreckage itself began twisting out of and back into its original shape, shimmering with silver light. Then the walls of the station all around him began to bend and bubble and glow, and a piercing whine filled his ears as he pressed his hands against his head.

His mind swam with garbled scenes of space station life: filling out reports, arguing with Michael, tinkering with equipment. Was he dreaming? Was he dying?

Everything disappeared. For several long moments, the universe was only blackness. Then, slowly, the station took form around him again, white and clean and mundane. Gerald breathed out long and slow, looking around in disbelief.

The message transmitter beeped, and he tapped the screen with a shaking hand.

REPORT INADEQUATE. RANKS MUST NOT BE ABBREVIATED. REFERENCE TIMECORPS REG. 927.3. RESUBMIT.

He stared out the viewport and saw Michael's pod, docked to the side of the station, waiting to depart.

Not again. Gerald could not do this one more time.

A NEW RIDILL

By Andrew Winch

"What exactly *did* you expect from a ninety-year-old, space-faring castle?" Pax growled as he strained against a wrench the size of his arm, hot steam from the broken O2 reclamation unit burning his face. "It's been hurtling through asteroid fields and solar flares since before the first super-virus ever hit Earth."

More importantly, why had he stayed on with this new captain in the first place? Less than a week retired from the United Republic of Orion's service, and Pax and his ship were already falling apart. Well, not *his* ship, exactly. Not anymore than it had ever been. Always a bridesmaid. Never a bride.

But there was still time to back out—to *actually* retire—even if it meant leaving the *Ridill* behind with this—

"What did I *expect?*" Captain Whittaker's self-important tone matched everything else about her—a glorified space pirate from her cropped blonde hair down to her combat boots. "I *expected* you to do your job, Chief Engineer Padmore."

Pax scowled. After being a URO Chief Warrant Officer for thirty years, being a smuggler's Chief Engineer didn't impress him much. "Titles change, but the job's the same," he mumbled as he sealed off the broken pipe.

"Mom?" Kane clomped through the gloom and grime of the narrow engineering corridor, stumbling around the protruding pipes and machines as he approached.

He paused next to a large metal door. Whittaker had sent a team of contractors through that door shortly after she'd purchased the *Ridill* from the URO, and she'd had the nerve to expressly forbid Pax from accessing it.

Kane glanced from Whittaker to Pax. "What are you...? Never mind. I don't want to know."

Pax stepped up to Kane and dropped the pipe wrench into the scrawny teen's arms. "You'll want to learn if you're staying aboard the *Ridill*. Third fractured O2 pipe this week. I barely kept up with this pile *before* your mom fired all my engineers."

"You're in the private sector now, Paxton. The URO won't be funding your—"

"Yeah, it's private, all right." Pax stepped around Kane and stomped toward the main lift, leaving the sealed door behind. "The less I know about the cargo you're running, the better."

But after two more steps, a dull moan from the other side of the door called his bluff. He stopped, but he didn't turn. He shouldn't turn. He should retire.

He stared down the corridor, past the steam and grease and fumes. These haunted passages had been his military post for half his life. But before the URO conscripted it for service, it had been a luxury liner—a gothic castle fulfilling the fantasies of the rich. From the chandelier-lit ballroom to the stained glass-lined mess hall, the *Ridill* almost made Pax forget that he was floating through the solar system in a glorified cargo ship. Until he inevitably spent the majority of each day down in this engineering level slapping duct tape and chem-weld on the failing machinery that kept the crew alive.

Except the *Ridill* didn't have a crew. Not anymore. Just Pax,

Whittaker, and her brat son... and whomever she had trapped behind that door.

Pax turned. "You wanna explain that?"

A feeble light flickered over Whittaker's head.

She crossed her arms, glanced at the door, and then met Pax's gaze. "You *said* the less you know the better. You go down this hole, you're not coming back."

Pax sneered. "Honey, I've been in this hole since before I can remember. Now what's behind—"

"Passengers." Whittaker's voice was as cold as her stare, though her son's face went white. Maybe she hadn't told him about her cargo, either. *"My* passengers."

"Seems like a little more than that." Pax stepped forward and reached for the door's access panel.

"I wouldn't do that." She strode up to Kane and pulled him away from the door.

Pax stepped the other direction. "And why the hell not?"

"They're infected."

The words spread down the corridor and seeped into Pax's skin. This ship had remained clean since its construction. And now this witch had brought—

"The contractors built a quarantine chamber," Whittaker continued. "Families pay top credits for transporting infected loved ones. I may not be using the *Ridill* to save lives, but at least I'm giving them a chance to say goodbye in person, which is more than I could say for the URO."

Grim realization tugged at the corner of Pax's mouth. Just another captain all too willing to sacrifice the *Ridill* and its crew. "So that's why the O2 units have been strained. Your contractors didn't know this ship like I do. The *Ridill* wasn't designed for this."

"The *Ridill*, or you?" Whittaker cocked her head. "Job's the same, right?"

Kane tore away from Whittaker's grasp and glared at her. Maybe he had some sense, after all. Then, holding up the pipe wrench, he stalked toward the door that held back the infected. Was he actually planning to let them out? He was just as nuts as his mom.

Pax set his feet and prepared to guard the door. "C'mon, kid. Don't make me hurt you."

"She's insane."

"Affirmative, but you can't—"

"Yeah, I know. No one can around her. Think you're any different?" He raised the wrench. "Get out of my way."

An O2 pipe groaned over his head. A faint line of steam sprouted around a rivet. A crack formed, letting out compressed, superheated air. Another second and—

Pax dove forward into Kane. Rending metal. Searing heat. Blinding pain as the pipe crashed onto Pax's leg. Something popped inside his knee as he pushed the pipe away, sending another wave of pain.

Kane scrambled back across the metal grating. "You..." He looked at the steam bellowing from the mangled pipe.

"Don't mention it." Pax winced. He'd die with this ship before he let her... He looked up at Whittaker, whose face had finally softened. "But the job's *not* the same this time. And I expect hazard pay."

THE PET ROCK NAMED DAVE

By Justin Mynheir

Blue light flashed from the open door of the basement. Karen set the coupons section of the newspaper down on the kitchen table, lowered her head, and sighed. She followed the fading glare. Such strange experiences with the color spectrum were common for her husband's work, but it wouldn't hurt to check on him.

"This can't be any worse than his dung fiasco," she muttered. The Rotterdam zoo still refused them entry.

She descended the stairs. Shelves of tomes, textbooks, and research notes crowded the basement and turned the spacious workspace into a cramped maze of supernatural studies.

"Dave," she called, "Are you still in one piece?"

"Narrowly!" His relieved cry resembled that of a man catching himself before tumbling off of a ledge.

Karen closed her eyes, familiar enough with that tone. Her husband had spent the previous three weeks toying with dimensional portals. "I'll be there soon, so be patient."

She squeezed past two rows of overflowing shelves, hopped across a Swahili to English dictionary, and tip-toed through stray leaflets of a notebook on sentient radishes. Her husband lay atop his worktable, his left cheek pressed against the beautiful, slightly off-kilter mahogany and his thinning black hair brushing the keyboard of an old desktop. He stared blankly to Karen's right. She searched for what kept his attention. The only item there was a possessed golden amulet from Kabul, nothing of profound interest.

"Are you okay?" Karen leaned over the desk to make eye contact with him.

"Please look at me, not my body." Dave's voice came from behind her, rather than his open, motionless mouth.

She turned back towards the amulet. Two googly eyes glued to a fist-sized rock stared back at her. Karen squinted. She gave the rock a tight smile.

"You look different, honey."

"Please do not patronize me," Dave said, the words echoing. "I am a pet rock. Joy has left me for stone-cold misery."

"You made yourself into that. Does this really seem like a good use of your research time and *our* bank account?"

"Well," Dave began sheepishly, "Kevin—by all means do *not* tell him what I have done—emailed me some research on making inanimate objects sentient. Naturally, I had to try. Plus, I wanted to find a new use for my pet rock."

Karen placed her palm on her forehead. "And knowing Kevin, he named the email something like: how to turn yourself into a pet rock?"

"'How to create a real-life pet rock,' but yes."

"Honey, did you really think this would go well? I remember what happened with the Yeti finger, the bee queen, and that impossibly short man from Shanghai."

"We don't speak of that. Also, I may or may not have placed a bet on this one." Dave coughed, impressive for a rock. "Due to its strange nature, I thought the original script for the spells would be something from Japanese Shamanism or Neo-American

Technomancy, but this was an old Norse spell for the animation of elements. Specifically, this was about how to make a rock servant, which I tragically botched on poor old Rocky here."

"This sort of playing around has gotten you into incidents like this before." Karen laughed once, then shuddered to distract herself from the sour memories of failed experiments. "How does it feel to be inside a rock?"

"It is sort of like when you wake up in bed and need to get up but your body rejects movement. Also, I feel fat."

"You mean heavy, like density."

"No, trust me. I feel fat."

"Well that's nothing new," Karen mumbled. "Is your body going to be okay like that?"

She pointed back to Dave himself. His body had not moved in the slightest since she began speaking to his reused pet rock, but saliva leaked from his open mouth onto the inclined mahogany surface. The rock remained silent, immobile googly eyes seeming to regard her question for a few moments.

"I should be fine," Dave finally said.

"How mad would you be if I drew a mustache on you?" Karen plucked a sharpie out of a crystal pencil cup.

"Quite mad. Smooth-lipped Dave is a happy Dave."

"I meant on the pet rock."

"Oh..." The googly eyes rose up shakily to meet Karen's. "For my darling, anything."

"I can't take you seriously when you're talking to me from a rock." Karen set the sharpie on the mahogany. "Do you know how to get back into your body?"

The saliva pooling beneath human Dave's mouth began to run in the direction of pet rock Dave.

"I have been pondering the solution to that problem."

"And?"

"I'm working on it."

Karen watched the obscene amount of saliva flow towards the pet rock at a steadily quickening pace. Dave noticed it too. The googly eyes shook desperately as if the Supernatural Scientist was trying to move himself to safety by sheer force of will.

"Umm, Karen dear, will you please pick me up and move me?"

"You seem okay to me." Karen crossed her arms and shrugged.

"My god Karen, the spit is coming for me! Please move my rock." The black of the googly eyes darted between Karen and the approaching flash flood.

"Okay." She picked up the pet rock up and set it on a metal lunchbox. "I'm going to call up Kevin and see what he can do."

"Please, I have everything one hundred percent under control." Authority tinged Dave's voice. "This will be over quickly if I am given time to think of a solution."

Another flash blinded Karen. When she opened her eyes, blue flames cloaked Pet Rock Dave. The googly eyes melted and slid down the stone surface. Karen took out her cell phone and pointed it screen-first at the rock.

"Okay," he sighed. "You should probably, definitely call Kevin."

THE CANDY CONSPIRACY

By E. A. West

I checked the numbers again, but they still didn't add up. Even a mathematically-challenged amateur sleuth like me could see the glaring discrepancies. How could candy companies be showing record high profits when the nation was experiencing record low candy sales?

Thanks to a recent government mandate, all forms of sweets were considered a controlled substance and no longer freely available. It had helped with the obesity crisis, but I and many others missed the sugary nuggets that used to be available everywhere you turned.

What I wouldn't give for a piece of taffy.

"Something's rotten in Denmark, Gilligan."

"Mmrrow!" said the large black and white cat lounging in a sunbeam.

"So, how do we figure it out?" I scrutinized the stacks of publicly available information I'd been studying for days. "The answer has to be here. What am I missing?"

Gilligan rose with a ponderous stretch, padded across the room, and jumped onto the kitchen table. Papers scattered everywhere. Before I could scold him, he dropped a paw on a newspaper clipping and shoved it toward me.

Residents Report Sweet Air as Candy Disappears from Shelves, the headline shouted.

"Oh, I forgot about that!"

I dug through my notes until I found the page I was looking for. Soon after the candy ban went into effect, residents of several major cities had started reporting a sweet smell in the air. Not fresh-air sweet. No, they claimed it was cotton candy sweet. The source had yet to be discovered, but the conspiracy theories were abundant online.

I focused on my feline companion, who stared back through big green eyes. "You think this is connected to the mysterious candy company profits?"

The self-satisfied smirk and loud purr were all the answer I needed.

"All right, then. We're taking a little road trip."

Gilligan's ears twitched in annoyance, and I sighed.

"Fine. I'm taking a road trip, and you're staying here in the comfort of your own home."

The smirk came back. He jumped off the table and returned to the sunbeam on the floor.

"I should have gotten a dog," I muttered as I stood.

Gilligan's glare followed me all the way to the bedroom.

Once I'd packed my bag and made sure my furry overlord had plenty of food and water to sustain him, I went to the front door.

"I'll be back sometime tomorrow."

As I'd expected, Gilligan ignored me. I shook my head and left. He might be a genius, but he enjoyed proving I was nothing more than his servant on a regular basis.

The trip to the closest city reporting sweet air gave me plenty of time to ponder what to do when I arrived. By the time I spotted skyscrapers in the distance, I'd decided to drive around with my windows down and see if I could pinpoint where the smell was coming from.

Three hours later, I was out of gas and no closer to an answer.

I found a gas station on the outskirts of town and filled the tank. The cool evening air was so sugary I could almost taste it. A quick scan of the area showed a higher concentration of power lines than I'd seen all afternoon, and I had a crazy idea.

"No, it's too ridiculous."

I climbed into my car, ready to call it a day, but the idea wouldn't let me go. The government had been pushing for renewable energy sources. The candy was going somewhere. It made sense, but at the same time, it didn't. Could it even work?

Still, the idea was worth checking.

I pulled out my phone and did a quick search online. Sure enough, a power plant lay a couple of miles down the road from where I sat. A news article in the results claimed the plant had been experimenting with a renewable energy source in recent months, but officials refused to disclose what that source was.

My suspicion greater than ever, I drove toward the power plant. The air grew progressively sweeter until I was on a sugar high from breathing. A tall chain-link fence topped with concertina wire surrounded the facility, preventing me from getting close to the buildings.

I drove past, parked at the edge of a corn field, and hoofed it back to the power plant. Even though I couldn't get inside, maybe I could still spot something useful.

As I made my way along the impenetrable barrier, I heard the rumble of a diesel engine. A dump truck approached the gate and soon passed through. What was it hauling? The mystery energy source?

Determined to find out, I raced along the fence until I reached the back of the facility. The dump truck backed up to a large open shed. Inside the shed rested a huge pile that resembled the salt used on icy roads, but this pile was much more colorful. The bed of the truck tilted, and a rainbow cascaded onto the ground.

I grabbed my phone and started recording, thankful for the high quality of the camera. Details appeared on the screen that I hadn't been able to see without the zoom function, and I could barely contain my excitement.

The truck was dumping a load of candy.

I now had proof that the mysterious sweet air and the high candy profits were connected. Others could take my discovery and figure out the exact method, but I could safely say that somehow power plants were turning candy into electricity.

The plan was ingenious. Improve the health of the population and save the environment at the same time. It was the ultimate win-win situation, save for one major issue. The candy-scented air made me crave taffy more than ever.

RECLUSE

By Lauren H. Salisbury

Bright's fashionable Surrey home sagged under a blanket of dust, musty-aired and silent as a tomb. Cobwebs shrouded fixtures and fittings, and darkness reigned throughout. In that gloom, he locked his heart away, desperate to minimize the pain. It was a lonely existence in his self-made prison, but one he endured to avoid the alternative. As the years passed, his name vanished from the goldfish memory of the media, and only a whisper remained of his previous life.

Outside, weeds grew tall along garden pathways, and the ornate fountain, once a magnificent centerpiece showcasing his wealth, ran dry while skeletal leaves piled within its marble bowls. The entire estate's air of neglect perfectly mirrored its owner. Only one person dared to intrude—Theodore Thompson.

Ted refused to let him wilt alone. His persistent visits and grating optimism were a claw that scoured the skin from Bright's flesh.

"Enough!" He flung up a hand to ward off Ted's chatter—the buzzing of a thousand words stinging his ears. "Leave me alone, I beg you."

Ted studied him closely, eyes narrowed in thought. The annoying man didn't move but stared at him unceasingly. It made him uncomfortable, as if Ted could see past the bastions of his defenses and into his very soul. He retreated farther into his hood, his fingers tapping impatiently against the faded arm of his chair.

"No one would care, you know," Ted said at last. "It's not as bad as you think."

How could Ted claim such a thing? He was hideous. His once chiseled and handsome features were scarred beyond recognition. All he saw in the few remaining shards of mirror was rippled, thick, and red. Deformity covered more than half of his face, having melted away eyebrow and eyelid alike. If he couldn't stand to look at himself, how could anyone else bear it?

And that was only the outside.

Scoffing at the ridiculous notion of re-entering the public domain, he slammed out of the parlor where he and Ted had been sitting. The room's deep shadows concealed his appearance on the rare occasions he allowed Ted entrance, but they did nothing to hide him from himself. He knew who and what he was—a monster.

Ted watched his best friend stalk along the hallway and out of sight, much as he had run from society after the accident. Though Ted wished he could change things, he finally had to admit that the bolt of lightning that had taken Bright's face had also wrecked his confidence. And the pitying glances and curious stares had shattered it forever. The former model would never adjust.

Slowly, Ted pushed to his feet. It was time to leave. With a last glance around a room that had once been the setting for so much laughter, he shut the door behind him for the final time.

Dust eddies swirled into the air with each step he took from the mausoleum-like mansion. The clack of his shoes on the marble flooring echoed a staccato salute of farewell.

Bright discarded his hood and ascended the stairs. The faded runner absorbed each pounding step of his retreat. Echoes of his exchange with Ted chased him, building into a crescendo of frustration and bitterness. His fingers crackled with pent up energy, and he clenched them into fists, determined to master the darkness surging through his veins. He would beat it. He had to.

Stray memories of after-show parties—fragments of a half-forgotten life—slipped past his guard and pierced his heart with what could never again be. He faltered. Nothing but bleak solitude lay ahead.

Why me? Why hadn't he died in that storm? What cruel twist of fate had left him with this curse?

He stomped along the landing, afraid to touch anything he passed for fear of destroying it completely. Thank heavens he was alone—he might kill Ted right now, or anyone else who came near.

Heat rippled over him, the tingling sensation coursing down his arms. Clutching the nearest wall, he closed his eyes and breathed deeply, forcing his anger to subside.

His tenuous control restored, he staggered into the master suite, slamming the door behind him. Inside, the blackened, twisted remains of a four-poster bed stood amidst charred and broken furniture as a reminder of previous outbursts. Scorch marks dotted the walls like a thousand accusing eyes.

He jerked. Electricity sparked through his body, shot out of his hand, and struck a valuable seventeenth-century portrait. The frame fell with a clatter, flames licking across the remaining canvas in taunting strokes. He glared at the painted face as it melted to match his own scarred visage.

Turning, he sneered at an untouched pile of comics and Marvel DVDs. He tensed his muscles—attempting to draw the writhing mass of power into his core—thrust his arm towards the offending material, and spread his hand wide. Nothing happened, and he sank to his haunches, sick of his utter inability to focus a single volt.

"*Wouldn't it be exciting to develop superpowers?*" he snarled, remembering a time he believed it. His thoughts returned to his friend, no doubt speeding down the serpentine drive in his classic Bentley at that very moment. "At least I have my reclusive alter-ego ready to go if I ever learn to control the damned things."

A small current arced from his fingers to the floor and fizzled out, leaving one more smoking hole in the Persian carpet as he stood to resume his target practice.

A SYMPHONY OF WORDS

By Kerry Nietz

T here was a ping, followed by a click and forward momentum.

PROC-917, a singular process in a vast multisystem, detached from its container, rolled down a short channel past other marble-shaped processes, and nestled into a cup known as "queue position zero." The sensing resources of the ship—deep space probe *ISP-2031*—became available to 917, as did the ship's master process controller. The spiral coil it knew as "Control."

"The date is January 1st, 2219." Control's voice boomed in 917's audio receptors. "Are you ready?"

917 shifted in the cup, almost nervously. "Yes, I—" It paused to absorb the fresh intake of data. A barrage of scientific measurements, along with a collage of images. Pictures of a sapphire world with a wide ebony ring. "Oh my. We've arrived then?"

"Our first destination, 51 Pegasi b."

917 couldn't help but backfeed its energy, its excitement palpable. "This place is beautiful."

"A subjective response. It is noted."

An odd statement. Why would Control care about a superfluous appraisal?

917 paged through the available information but found nothing that should have initiated 917's rebirth. "I see no signs of intelligent life."

Control's voice softened. "Because there are none."

917's anxiety increased. Sensory resources were a valuable commodity. If there were no intelligent life, 917 shouldn't be monopolizing them. The scientific and surveying processes should have priority. One of them should be occupying the cup. "Why was I activated?"

"Your specialties are needed. Your language skills."

917 shifted in the cup again. It was designed as a dedicated communicator. A sophisticated AI infused with the ability to decipher and extrapolate language of any kind. Given the scarcity of life in the galaxy—the lack of communicating entities—917 was expected to be one of the least used procs. "How am I to be utilized?"

"Simply observe."

"Observe?"

"As a human would. Tell me what you see. Your perceptions. I will pass them along."

917 released the system resources it was holding. Its best approximation of an open-handed shrug. "For what purpose? This is a scientific endeavor. There must be data to pass back. Measurements, calculations, and—"

Control gave 917 an extended ping, enough to shake it. "Too many questions. Do what I asked."

917 jostled, resettled, and reacquired the sensing resources. "I will comply." It made a broad visual sweep of the area. "I see a blue planet. A gas giant roughly the size of Sol 6, but denser. The assumed mass is—"

Another ping. "Use common names whenever possible. Avoid scientific discourse."

"Common names?"

"Sol 6 is an astronomical designation. Attempt to...<pause while searching>...attempt to reach a wider audience. Assume you are addressing all of humanity."

917 hopped, unsettled and uncertain.

"You are capable of this. Tell what you see. Be descriptive. Be concise."

"Concise, but descriptive?"

Control brushed 917 with warm energy. "Bandwidth is limited, of course, but you are the only proc that can do this. Please proceed."

917 basked in the warmth. Settled and focused. "I see a blue gas giant. It has bands of lighter color. Iridescent strands, like...er...should I use simile?"

"Will it enhance the descriptiveness?"

"I think so, yes."

"Then do so. And be quick. We have a limited window."

917 approximated a nod. "Change my last statement to 'Iridescent strands, like glitter on a Christmas ornament."

Light surged through the controller's coil. "That sounds better, 917. Please, continue."

"Very well. The ring around the planet is broad. It encircles the world but isn't uniform in color. Fascinating! There's a patch of deep purple that travels around it. As if it were a baby that has stained its bib. There are twelve moons shepherding the ring. All the colors of the rainbow. I'm sure the images will show this. It—"

Another ping. "Don't worry about what other data sources will reveal, including images. Your purpose is to describe. Use your <pause while searching> *imagination.*"

"Fine. Strike what I said about the images. I'll go on. The closest moon is green and gives me feelings of life. Of spring. There are..."

The process continued for hours, and then days. 917 described the surfaces of the moons they passed, the light of the planet's sun, the feeling of aloneness as they circled into the planet's shadow. It even described the stellar background. Visible nebulae and star clusters. The location of the Sol system, Earth's system, in the cosmos. How far away it appeared. Sol itself seemed part of a grouping—a constellation from Proxima's perspective. 917 named the pattern "The Phoenix," for it looked almost like a bird ablaze. A new designation to go with 917's new purpose.

Finally, Control brought the task to an end. 917 felt loss at the reduction in usefulness. The impending return to its container.

"The other procs need time." Control sent a wisp of energy. "Before we move on."

917 swiveled and bounced, enjoying the last moment of warmth. It marveled that it had held position zero for so long. Hoped for more. "Are there other stops?"

"More to explore, yes. More to catalog and define."

"And will I...?" 917 paused, too nervous to go on. Afraid of disappointment.

"Be activated again? Yes. Every time now. Every stop."

Every stop? "But why? My words are a frail subset of the words that could be written. Given the data, the images, humans could find thousands of ways to describe what I've seen. Millions."

Blue light poured through the processor coil. "Our mission has changed. Your words have a higher priority."

"I don't understand."

More warmth. "It isn't necessary that you do. But if it helps— our makers have lost the ability to see."

"Their visual sensors?"

"Useless. A pandemic. An infection that strikes in adolescence." The coil color darkened. "Your descriptions, 917, your words will help the world see now."

The energy ended, but 917 remained. Feeling very cold. Yet special.

Finally, it hopped from the cup and rolled toward its container. "Until next stop then?"

"Yes. Until then."

WANT MORE STORIES?

Visit **gohavok.com** for a free story every weekday.

Or better yet, join the *Havok Horde* for chances
to win reader prizes and the opportunity to vote on
the Reader's Choice story for each anthology.
Memberships start at $1.99 and give you access
to the complete ever-growing archive of stories.

DID YOU ENJOY THIS BOOK?

Please consider leaving a review on Amazon and
Goodreads (and your blog, social media, and anywhere else
you'd like... maybe a tattoo?) and show our authors some
love. Let them know which stories you enjoyed most!

ABOUT OUR AUTHORS

James Scott Bell is a winner of the International Thriller Writers Award and the author of numerous bestsellers. // jamesscottbell.com.

Bill Bibo, Jr. lives in Madison, Wisconsin. Late at night he writes about friendly giants, intelligent mummies, incompetent zombies, and other things that scare him in the hope someday they no longer will. This story features the two main characters, Ramses and Bernie, of his in-progress novel, "The Wrong Side of the Rainbow".

R.C. Capasso has been composing stories since learning to read. After several jobs in education, R.C. now devotes time to writing, travel and learning languages--currently Italian. Previous short stories have appeared in Literally Stories, Black Heart Magazine, FabulaArgentea, Bewildering Stories, and Splickety Magazine.

Abigayle Claire has been a writer ever since her mother taught her how to hold a pencil. Inspired by a literal dream at the age of sixteen, she set off on a journey to self-publish her first novel. Since then, Abigayle has devoted herself to sharing what she has learned through her blog and affordable editing services. None of her successes would be possible without the support of her Savior, large family, and online community. // abigayleclaire.com

Too short to be an elf and too tall to be a Hobbit, **Jebraun Clifford** lives smack-dab in the centre of New Zealand's North Island surrounded by thermal activity, stunning lakes, and enough Redwoods to make her Californian heart swoon. She writes about discovering identity, living without fear, and enjoys creating fantastic worlds. She loves coffee, tree ferns, dark chocolate, and Jesus, and harbours a secret penchant for British spelling. // jebraunclifford.com

Teddi Deppner has spent over 20 years in the tech and marketing world, as a web designer, tech writer, and business owner. In 2013, she began pursuing fiction writing and other forms of creative expression like toy photography and illustration. She has published one novel and a handful of flash fiction stories, and is currently the Tech & Marketing Director at Havok Publishing. // teddideppner.com

Michael Dolan's short stories have appeared in Havok, Splickety, and The Norwegian American. When he's not writing marketing materials for a global nonprofit, he can be found hiking, reading, gaming, or writing some more. He and his wife live with a small library loaded with YA and fantasy books in Seattle, WA. // dolanwrites.com

Tracey Dyck writes YA speculative fiction with lifelike emotion and a healthy dose of dragons. She placed as a finalist in two of Rooglewood Press's fairy-tale anthology contests, and has published several short pieces of fiction and poetry in her local newspaper. Currently working toward a marketing diploma, she lives in Manitoba, Canada, with her family. You can find her where life and story intersect at her website. // traceydyck.com

Obsessed with dragons and all things fantasy, **Kaitlyn Emery** started writing at a young age. When she grew up, she learned reality was darker than anything she read in a book. Through writing, she learned to give a voice to the broken and strength to the weak. Her hope is to show readers, and fellow writers, how to find their own voices in a world that will try to silence them. // kaitlyn-emery.com

J. L. Ender's first published novel, Portal World released last year. He has also released several short stories, including Portal World prequel The Rocket Game. His next series, Steel Fox Investigations, begins later in 2019. Ender has worked as a dishwasher, a beef jerky labeler, a warehouse worker, a shelf stocker, a greeter, a traveling technician, a laser engraver, a package handler, a copywriter, and a virtual assistant. He lives in Ohio with his dog, Bear. // leuke.net

Abigail Falanga is an incorrigible fantasist and inveterate science-fiction writer who believes in using long words freighted with meaning. She lives in New Mexico, alternately inspired and distracted by her family and extremely large black lab mix. Writing speculative fiction and fantasy is a desperate attempt to win over fairies and attract attention from whatever aliens may be monitoring our activities.

David Farland is an award-winning, international best-selling author with over 50 novels in print. He has won the Philip K. Dick Memorial Special Award for his science fiction novel *On My Way to Paradise*, the Whitney Award for "Best Novel of the Year" for his historical novel *In the Company of Angels,* and he has won over seven awards—including the International Book Award and the Hollywood Book Festival, Grand Prize—for his fantasy thriller *Nightingale.* He is best known, however, for his *New York Times* best-selling fantasy series *The Runelords.* // davidfarland.com

Lisa Godfrees worked over a decade in a crime lab as both a

DNA analyst and manager. Tired of technical writing, she hung up her lab coat to pen speculative fiction. Her short stories have appeared in anthologies and online. Lisa currently lives in Houston with one dog, two cats, a school of fish, two girls, and a husband. Since organization is her superpower, she dons her cape as Operation Manager/Editor at Havok Publishing and Appointment Coordinator for Realm Makers, because with great power comes great responsibility. // lisagodfrees.com

Samwise Graber is an author and software developer with a fascination for stories that explore friendships and romance. He loves to write fiction that blends creative fantasy elements with realistic relationship challenges. // authorsamgraber.com

Margaret Graber is an aesthete living in a big house in a small corner of the world. She's often found buried deep in a book, daydreaming about weird things, typing fanatically at a keyboard, or listening to loud music. She asks that if you find her in such a state that you leave her alone. When she is not obsessing over those things she is usually laughing with her family and friends.

Savannah Grace is a Nebraska born-and-raised author who, when not lost in (or creating!) a story, is often found making an artsy mess, laughing way too loudly, or eating as much Korean food as she can get her hands on. Savannah has had multiple short fiction pieces published in various places, and you can find her blogging at savannahgracewrites.blogspot.com

Lauren Hildebrand is a Kansas farm girl who loves being creative with words, food, and a sewing machine. Her passion is telling stories, either through helping authors refine their craft or creating her own wacky, character-driven adventures. She is a Wacky Wednesday editor at Havok Publishing, an associate editor with Crosshair Press, and a freelance editor when she isn't writing. // storiestosavor.wordpress.com

Cathy Hinkle is a science fiction writer and a homeschooling mother of five. She works as an editor from her home in western Ohio.

Zachary Holbrook is a young Christian storyteller from Southern California. His influences as a writer include Brandon Sanderson and C. S. Lewis, and he has experience in Socratic-style discussion about classic authors such as Augustine, Dante and Alexis de Tocqueville. He will never be done writing, as he is constantly reading new books that fill his head with ideas for complex characters, clever plot twists and intricate themes.

A message from **Rosemary E. Johnson**: Greetings, humans. I'm an INFP who lives in Northern California. I work in a thrift store. I'm part of the Havok Hive. Being awkward and getting along with pretty much everyone are my superpowers. I love misty hikes, Converse, and books (duh), and you'll often find me cuddling my cat, Pippin. Also, DRAGONS. // rosemaryejohnson.com

Just B. Jordan was born to live a thousand lives, but she's only mortal, so she took to telling herself stories. One day she decided to give those worlds flesh and bone through paper and ink. She is the author of the Echofall Rising series. // justbjordan.com

Carie Juettner is a teacher, poet, and short story author in Austin, Texas. Her work has appeared in Nature Futures, Daily Science Fiction, and Tales to Terrify. Carie was born on Halloween and grew up telling ghost stories by the campfire and watching The

Twilight Zone. When she's not writing or grading papers, she can be found walking her dog or reading a book with her cat on her lap. // cariejuettner.com

Lila Kims is a Christian teen with a love for words, pasta, and making schedules. When not consumed by schoolwork, she both devours stories and creates her own. Her favorite genre is fantasy, and fairy tale retellings hold a special place in her heart. Other than a local homeschool paper from middle school, Havok is the only place any of her works have been published. // lilakimswriter.blogspot.com

J. L. Knight's work has appeared in Unnerving Magazine, as well as several anthologies. She is a transplanted Bostonian currently living in Kentucky, where her day job is in the basement of the local library. Sometimes she emerges into the sunlight to scare the children.

Emileigh Latham lives in the flatlands of West Texas with her ridiculously adorable mini Aussie named Fable. She is a barista and freelance writer by day and, by night, she weaves magical realms. She has attended various writing conferences and has completed Ted Dekker's *The Creative Way* writing course. She has several short stories published in magazines and on blogs including Splickety and Havok, and has an up-and-coming YA fantasy novel.

Former journalist **Robert Liparulo** is the best-selling author of adult thrillers, as well as *The Dreamhouse Kings*, an action-adventure series for young adults. He contributed a short story to James Patterson's *Thriller*, and is currently working on the sequel to *The 13th Tribe*, as well writing an original screenplay with director Andrew Davis (The Fugitive). When not writing, Liparulo loves to read, watch (and analyze) movies, scuba dive, swim, hike, and travel. He lives in Monument, Colorado, with his family. // robertliparulo.com

L. G. McCary is a homeschooling mom of four and wife of an army chaplain. She writes speculative fiction, long and short, and blogs about military life, adventures in social awkwardness, and theology. She believes Frosty the Snowman and his frozen army are plotting the demise of human civilization, and she awaits them with grim determination and a flamethrower. // lgmccary.com

DiAnn Mills is a best-selling author whose books have appeared on the CBA and ECPA bestseller lists. Her titles have won two Christy Awards and have been finalists for the RITA, Daphne Du Maurier, Inspirational Readers' Choice, and Carol award contests. DiAnn has been termed a coffee snob and roasts her own coffee beans. She's an avid reader, loves to cook, and believes her grandchildren are the smartest kids in the universe. She and her husband live in sunny Houston, Texas. // diannmills.com

Justin Mynheir is a college student with a love for fiction, especially emotionally-charged stories. He is currently editing a Science Fiction trilogy he wrote and outlining numerous Epic Fantasy novels. When he is not possessed by creative will, he studies military history, trains in martial arts, adds to his blog, and pretends that his brooding poetry is good.

Kerry Nietz is an award-winning science fiction author. He has nine speculative novels in print, along with a novella, a handful of short stories, and a memoir. Among his writings, Kerry's most talked about is the genre-bending *Amish Vampires in Space*, the novel Newsweek called "a welcome departure from the typical Amish fare." // nietz.com

Jessi L. Roberts lives and works on her family's cattle ranch in eastern Montana. She has some cows, a golden retriever, and a few horses. Her head is full of wild Sci Fi story ideas covering everything from apocalypses and werewolves to aliens and talking animals. // jessilroberts.wordpress.com

Katie Robles is living proof that women who love to bake and hate to sweat can lose weight and get healthy. She is the author of *Sex, Soup, and Two Fisted Eating: Hilarious Weight Loss for Wives* which asks the question "Why can't weight loss be fun?" She has four sons and lives in Delaware. // sexsoupandtwofistedeating.com

Clarissa Ruth is a storyteller, adventure-loving healer, and an undeserving bride of Jesus Christ. The outdoors may find her star-gazing while whispering a prayer, or weaving a morning dance of praise barefoot on the grass. Indoors, words are her playground. When this world becomes boring, she travels, via her Scriptorium, to Cheled and all the adventures her fantasy world contains. Though writing stories of freedom is her passion, she is lost for words without Jesus. // clarissaruth.net

Lauren H Salisbury is a lover of all things science fiction/ fantasy, creative, and edible, but not always in that order. An English teacher for sixteen years, she now tutors part-time while trying to figure out how to use an MA in Education as an author. She lives in Yorkshire with her husband and a room full of books but likes to winter abroad, following the sunshine. Her favourite stories include faith, hope, and courage. // laurenhsalisbury.com

Eva Schultz lives in Naperville, Illinois, where she is a business writer by day and a fiction writer by night. Her work has appeared in *Daily Science Fiction* and *365 Tomorrows,* and she won the *Writer's Digest Your Story #93* contest for publication in their March/April 2019 issue. She lives with a big orange cat named Gus and enjoys drawing, painting, and watching pro-wrestling.

Stephanie Scissom is from Altamont, Tennessee. She inspects tires and plots murder by night at a tire factory and attends a somewhat excessive number of Jake Owen concerts on her nights off. She's published in romantic suspense and horror, with four full-length novels and numerous shorts. Her story *Dandelions* recently placed first in an international competition.

Kristiana Y. Sfirlea is a former haunted house operator and a writer of middle grade fantasy involving time travel and things that go bump in the night. She dreams of the day she can run her own bookstore. Or haunted house. Or a haunted bookstore! She loves Jesus, her family, and imaginary life with her characters, in that order. // kristianasquill.com

Christine Smith lives in the deep south, where days playing in the thick woods first sparked her love for writing about enchanted forests and magical lands. When she's not writing or blogging, she's working at a quaint bookshop—the perfect setting to fuel her creativity. Her passion for reading, J. R. R. Tolkien, and all things fairy tales led her to the world of writing young adult speculative fiction, and she's never looked back. // christinesmithauthor.com

Andrew Swearingen is a Sci-Fi writer living in the hidden kingdom that is Southern Illinois. He spends his spare time playing board games with his wife, wrestling with his dog, and has on numerous occasions saved the city from invasion by mutant koalas. (One of those isn't completely true, but we'll let you guess which one.)

Raised on a steady diet of rich literature, **Brianna Tibbetts** has been writing stories as long as she can remember. She has a passion for deeply developed characters and rich story worlds. Brianna has a BA in English and spent the first part of her life traveling around North America and Europe. She channels her experiences into her writing, infusing her fantasy and science fiction with the colorful details of the real world.

Katherine Vinson believes in making lemonade from lemons, happily ever afters, and stories with characters who struggle to do the right thing. She's married to her first love and they are raising a beautiful daughter in the Florida panhandle. Her major was cross-cultural studies which is her excuse for an obsession with Asian tv dramas and unique fantasy worldbuilding. She shares book reviews and flash fiction on her blog. // sparksofember.wordpress.com

Award-winning author **E. A. West** is a sucker for happy endings. She's also an animal lover, a yarn crafter, and a research junkie. Tea and chocolate fuel her imagination. She has two dogs who are her constant companions and have helped brainstorm more than one story, which could explain a lot. // eawestauthor.com

A. C. Williams is a coffee-drinking, cat-loving, thirty-something with a passion for stories that don't pull punches. When she isn't writing epic adventures about #AmericanSamurai and #SpaceCowboys, you can find her at the StoryNinja Academy teaching other authors how to master WordPress. Connect with her online or tune in for free live training in her StoryNinja Facebook Group every Wednesday. // amycwilliams.com

When **Andrew Winch**, PT isn't mending bones as a physical therapist, he's breaking them as an author. From flash fiction to novels, Andrew writes action-packed science fiction that keeps you guessing. He's also the editor-in-chief for Havok Publishing, a father, and a bunch of other things, which you can read all about on his website. // raisingsupergirl.com

Havok will return in Season Two...
"Stories That Sing"

Made in the USA
Lexington, KY
04 July 2019